THE TRAIL DRIVE

G·K
Hall
&Co.

Also by Lauran Paine
in Large Print:

The Arizona Panhandle
Death Was the Echo
Apache Trail
Death of a Millionaire
Man from Butte City
The Mustangers
Wilderness Road
Cache Canyon
High Ridge Range
The Killer Gun
Murder in Paradise
Murder without Motive
Trail of the Freighters
The Grand Ones of San Ildefonso
Murder Now, Pay Later

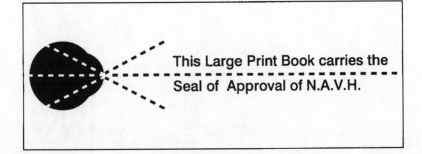

This Large Print Book carries the
Seal of Approval of N.A.V.H.

THE TRAIL DRIVE

Lauran Paine

G.K. Hall & Co. • Thorndike, Maine

Published in 2000 by arrangement with Golden West Literary Agency.

G.K. Hall Large Print Paperback Series.

The text of this Large Print edition is unabridged.
Other aspects of the book may vary from the original edition.

Set in 16 pt. Plantin by Rick Gundberg.

Printed in the United States on permanent paper.

Library of Congress Cataloging-in-Publication Data

Paine, Lauran.
    The trail drive / Lauran Paine.
      p. cm.
    ISBN 0-7838-9280-2 (lg. print : sc : alk. paper)
    1. Cattle drives — Fiction. 2. Large type books. I. Title.
PS3566.A34 T72 2000
813′.54—dc21   00-061470

THE TRAIL DRIVE

1

Seventeen Hundred Head

According to Bruce Cutler who had sold the herd to Donald Bright there was a quicker way to reach the lower Florence Basin than by following the usual drover's trail south from Cutbank.

Because Donald Bright was anxious to return to the home-place five miles from Antelope in Florence Basin in time for his daughter's wedding, he sent his rangeboss Burt Sommers to hunt up Bruce Cutler and get the particulars, then Bright had taken the evening stage out of Cutbank straight south. His last words to Burt Sommers were direct enough. "Take the short cut and get the drive down to the ranch as quick as you can."

Burt found Bruce Cutler at the saloon in Cutbank that same night before supper. He went alone because seventeen hundred head of bred cows required his four riders out at the bedground.

Cutler was an oddly shaped individual, very obese through the gut and rear, but otherwise about normal. He was a broker, not an owner, and like all livestock brokers, Cutler was shrewd, clever, quick with figures and with a fine predatory instinct. He had arranged the sale of the bred cows, had steered it through to its satisfactory conclusion, had Donald Bright's bank draft in his pocket and would take it out to the seller in a day or two, and skim his high percentage off the top.

He was in an expansive mood when Burt found him. They had one drink then went down to the cafe and Cutler ordered a steak large enough to overlap a platter, a side platter of fried spuds, a pot of coffee, and apple cobbler. Burt had coffee, spuds and a much smaller steak, and as Cutler explained about the short cut he waved his knife and fork.

"Used it myself a couple of times an' while it ain't easy, bein' through the mountains and all, it'll sure shave time off your drive. You go south from Cutbank until you find a marker-tree, an old bull-pine, with a big broad blaze on it, and you'll see the old trail. Overgrown now because modern drovers ain't got the grit to use it any more, but it's wide an' part of the time you'll be travellin' through canyons so's the cattle cain't get away from you on either side." Cutler chewed a huge mouthful of steak for a while before completing what he had to say. "There's a river about three, four days out. Cuts right across a broad canyon. Lots of feed there. This time o' year you can ford it easy. I don't know the name of it — I did know it, but I forgot.

Seems like it was Simas River or something like that.

"After you cross the river the country gets better — more grass and browse. From there on you got about three more days an' you'll hit the north flat of Florence Basin. Mister Sommers, young fellers like yourself an' your crew — hell — you can make that trip ridin' sidesaddle, and save three, four days." Cutler's broad, round face curled into a smile that nearly hid his shrewd, hard little blue eyes. "Might even make it in time for the weddin' of Mister Bright's daughter . . . Say, that Mister Bright's a mon-eyed man, ain't he? Wrote out that draft with a real flourish, wears hand-made boots and a gold buckle and all. Fine specimen of a cowman, I'd say."

Burt pushed his plate away, empty, pulled in his coffee cup and regarded the broker with interest. That steak, two-thirds demolished now, had weighed about two pounds and it had been cooked rare. "How's the feed between here and that river?" he asked watching Cutler gorge.

The broker gestured again with his fork-hand. "Good. As far as I know ain't no one used that old trail for years. Like I said — drovers nowa-days got to have flat country and open land all around, like they was drivin' milk cows to the barn. It ain't *real* good, but for grazin' along it's plenty good." Cutler pushed away the gory rem-nants of his steak and pulled in the platter of fried potatoes, pausing only briefly to rinse out with black coffee, then continued speaking. If there was one thing a successful livestock broker was good at, it was talking persuasively, even when he did not have to.

"I brought up three thousand razorbacks nine years ago and s'help me, believe it or not, them slab-sided animals gained weight." Cutler paused with potatoes half way to his mouth to look steadily at the younger, taller and leaner man. "The way I used to drive cattle through that sort of country was to let 'em graze it off as they went, and never stop until I found real good feed." He gulped the potatoes and grinned around them. "Mister Sommers, a feller like you'll make that drive hands down. By any chance you from Texas?"

Burt finished his coffee. "Kansas."

"Sure enough? By gawd, y'know I was born out there and grew up near Lawrence, Kansas. That was back when they called 'er bloody Kansas. That'd be before your time."

Burt leaned to arise. "I heard the old tales, Mister Cutler. My paw and two uncles went through them."

"Not me, Mister Sommers. I could sense which way the wind was blowin' so I went over into Missouri, along the river, and let those idiots fight it out. It was silly anyway. I got my start tradin' up and down the river, before I come out here."

As Burt arose Bruce Cutler paused, an implement in each hand. He put down the knife and shoved out a paw. "Good luck, Mister Sommers. And I'll tell you something, your boss got a good buy on them cows. They're as good a bunch of poppin' redbacks as you could find anywhere. Bred to up-graded redback bulls. He just about stole 'em, for a fact."

Burt pumped the hand once, nodded and walked out of the cafe into some cool, fresh air. Around him, Cutbank was lighted, with wide gaps between lights, there was a sweet scent of woodsmoke in the star-bright night, and as he headed for the liverybarn to get his horse and head for the bed-ground, a very pretty girl with jet-black hair, eyes to match, and skin the colour of new cream, studied him as they approached, each walking in the opposite direction, and when Burt looked up, she faintly smiled and kept on walking.

His boot-steps dragged a yard or two. He looked back. She had as pretty a swinging walk as he had ever seen, but she did not slacken gait nor turn, so he continued on in the direction of the barn, and down there, with a pair of guttery old carriage lamps on either side of the doorway, he looked back again. But she was gone.

The nighthawk came up expectantly. "That big bay with the DB on his left shoulder?"

Burt nodded and looked northward again. Her face had been a pure cameo. Maybe the darkness cleared up any flaws, if she'd had any. When the hostler brought his horse he turned it once, swung up, and rode out.

11

All the way out to the bed-ground he thought of that girl. She was fixed in his mind, and hell, he'd only had that one look at her. It had lasted, at the most five or six seconds.

By the time he saw flickering camp-light he knew he would never forget that girl as long as he lived. He'd carry that cameo-picture in his memory, and also in his heart, until he died.

Jack and Sut were out, Morgan and Pete were smoking up close to the little dry-wood fire. They watched him ride in, nodded, watched him ride out to care for his horse, and one of them pitched another piece of scavenged wood upon the fire, sparks sputtered, and somewhere from a fair distance a man's whistling reached back. Morgan, who was a tall, spare, bony man with flat high cheekbones, black hair and dark eyes, dumped his quirley into the fire and said, "I wonder did he bring back a bottle?"

Sut Sutherland was a shorter, thicker man with grey at the temples and squint lines at the outer corner of each eye from years at his trade. "Of course he did," he said in a tone which left no room for doubt.

Sut was right. When Burt arrived at the fire he handed Morgan a bottle, sank down and told them what the livestock broker had told him. Morgan passed the bottle to Sut and fished for the makings of another smoke as he said, "Where is this blaze-tree?"

"South. You can scout for it on ahead in the morning, Morg, once we get the cattle moving.

12

Maybe a couple of miles. You find it and wait down there. Signal back."

Sut offered the bottle to Burt, who refused it so Sut placed it very carefully among some firewood for the men to find when they came in off night-watch. Sut said, "Damned good bunch of cows, Burt. We rode around 'em a few times after those hired hands of Mister Cutler's headed back for town."

Burt was interested. "Any of them real springy?"

Sut shrugged and looked at Morgan. "I didn't notice any that was close, did you?"

Morgan shook his head. "No, but then I didn't look at every cow either. I think what Cutler said was the truth — they was all bred within a couple of months of one another. Anyway, I didn't see any I thought might calve on the drive south."

Burt sat in thoughtful silence. He had driven herds before, but not within the past six years since he'd been rangeboss for Bright's big DB outfit in Florence Basin. But that did not trouble him. He did not know the country they were going into; that did not bother him either, but he thought about it. Still, any late springtime with warm rains falling every week or so, even the high country had grass growing behind every tree and from beneath every rock, and that was the main consideration; the cattle could graze along. As for rough country, he, his riders, and presumably the cattle, had seen plenty of that before.

2

Something To Worry About

They had them moving just at sunup, and although being calvy did not show very much among the cows, they were already beginning to act like heavy cows — slow, stolid, unexcitable as long as no one pushed them.

Pete Smith passed Burt Sommers at a dead walk and said, "These here are the kind I like to trail."

Burt nodded, watched Pete sashay eastward to bring some drifters back to the main bunch, and privately agreed. If a man had to drive cattle it was better if they had most of the Texas razorback bred out of them, had shorter horns and legs, and more heft to go with less flighty dispositions. He looped his reins, watched Morgan lope far ahead on his way down to find the blaze-tree, cocked an eye at the springtime sun in its pale setting of flawless sky, and built a smoke.

They had Cutbank on their east side for a while, then it began to fall away to the rear. The land was largely open for a few miles before mountains pushed in closer on both sides making a sort of long grassy funnel of the flat land. Due southward, following down through the funnel, which was crooked and about a mile wide, was the traditional drover's trail southward.

As Burt slouched along he thought that since the new cows did not have to go to the bulls there was no real reason for Mister Bright to want them to arrive in Florence Basin quickly. But Mister Bright, while a pleasant man to work for, was one of those impatient, high-strung, incisive individuals. He would not have been worth a damn on a drive like this. He would be one of those men who would wear out three or four horses every day sashaying back and forth after every cow that got a hundred feet from the main drive.

Burt rolled and lit a smoke as the rising sun warmed his back and side, watched the obedient big bunch of redbacks plod along, in no hurry, cropping a mouthful of grass now and then. There was no dust yet; the dew had not evaporated. Jack Dineen was on the west side where the flat country began to squeeze in. Over to the west Pete Smith was easing along. Pete was a great hand to sing. He did not have a bad voice, but probably even if he'd had one it would not have discouraged him very much; he liked to sing as he rode along.

Sut Sutherland was up at point, staying a hundred or so yards ahead of the lead cows, one foot dangling out of the stirrup, enjoying himself and

15

still keeping a good watch.

It was a good crew. Sut was oldest, but Morgan probably was close to the same age as Sut, but Morgan being a 'breed did not show his age as much, and he was tall, lanky, loose-moving, more like a younger man. He had a sense of humour, they all did, in their business they had to have, but Morg was also taciturn at times, particularly when he was around people he did not know. He was the best roper among them, but Jack Dineen, the youngest among them, was the best all-around tophand.

Burt punched out his smoke atop the saddlehorn, watched how the mountain closed in on both sides, and finally saw the flash of sunlight off something shiny to indicate that Morgan was up ahead.

Burt left his drag position to lope far out and around and get down to the blaze-tree where Morgan was hunkering in bull-pine shade smoking, patiently watching and waiting. When Burt swung up and dismounted Morgan arose and pointed to an overgrown but distinctly discernible old trail at his back.

Burt nodded. "You look it over?"

"For a mile or so," replied the lanky 'breed. "As far as I went it looks all right. Boulders been washed off the slopes into the trail here and there, and not much grass, but I've seen worse trails." Morgan turned back to gaze up where the on-coming herd was finally beginning to raise a little dust. "Saw some fresh barefoot

16

horse tracks up in there, crossin' from the west to the east." When he finished speaking Morgan turned his black gaze calmly back to the rangeboss.

Burt said, "How many?"

And as Morgan replied they were both thinking the same thing; Reservation jumpers. Probably just meathunters but when Indians left the reservation they were breaking the law and they knew it. Bronco redskins usually had their backs up before they jumped the reservation. They could be very troublesome.

"Morg; how many?"

"Maybe a dozen. I'd guess they crossed the trail maybe yesterday."

Burt lifted his eyes to the heights of the hills on both sides of the trail. What Cutler had said about narrow canyons being ideal places to drive cattle through was correct as far as it went, but while he stood there looking along the saw-tooth skyline Burt was thinking of something else. Being down in a canyon was not the best place to be if there were broncos on horseback in the vicinity.

Morgan guessed the younger man's thoughts and offered a suggestion. "I can scout along on the heights. It's probably nothing. Just some redskins who want to go to some old ceremonial ground, or something."

Burt sighed. His orders were to take the shortcut. Maybe Morgan was right too. Hell, there hadn't been any worthwhile skirmishes with Indians in ten years. He nodded his head. "Yeah, you do that — but Morg, be damned careful."

The placid, expressionless dark face showed a crooked small smile as Morgan replied to the admonition. "I'm always careful, Burt."

"Let's get the leaders pointed down through here first, then you can break off and go up there."

Sut rode up with a lazy wave, still riding with one foot kicked loose and called ahead. "How's it look?"

Morgan and Burt swung into the saddle to position themselves athwart the regular trail and block the cattle from going ahead that way. Burt sang out to Sut. "All right. Overgrown and maybe a little rough, but all right . . . Swing 'em, Sut."

There was a brief scuffling and piling up as the leaders halted, peering around to see what was required of them. They might have hung there longer but the pressure from behind pushed them ahead. They turned off the main trail and walked past the old bull-pine, and now there was more dust as seventeen hundred four-footed critters churned and fidgeted until the leaders were well along and the drive could string out again.

Morgan was on the far side. He waited until he was certain Burt was watching, then wig-wagged with his hat, turned and rode off through the underbrush and pine trees towards the lower slopes.

18

Burt remained athwart the main trail, not because he expected any break-aways to push onward in that direction, but to await the arrival of Jack Dineen who had been flagging to the west of the herd. When Jack rode up, adjusting a neckerchief over his nose and mouth because of the dust, his very fair complexion was already beginning to show the coppery colour it got every summer. He halted beside Burt, lowered the rag and said, "That don't look like much of a trail to me."

Burt relayed what Morgan had said, but without mentioning the barefoot horse tracks, and Jack frowned over where the cattle were trudging like a red wave past the blaze-tree. "Hope to hell we don't get a flash-flood while we're down in there."

Burt cast a glance skyward. "We won't," he replied. "You better move along."

Jack pulled up his face cloth and reined away. Burt caught an occasional glimpse of Pete Smith over the herd, then he too disappeared down into the overgrown trail and Burt went calmly around to pick up the drag and keep it moving, although there really was no need, the cows were perfectly willing to follow those ahead.

By noon, the DB riding crew discovered something Cutler had neglected to mention to Burt Sommers: When the late springtime sun got directly overhead, and perhaps because there was no place for the heat to go, being blocked on both sides by those stiffly rising

19

mountains, it got as hot as the hubs of hell down in there.

But at least there was much less dust. Aside from stands of underbrush and grass, both of which were pulverized as the herd stolidly plodded over them, the ground was gravelly.

Fortunately, there was no lack of water. Sidehill freshets made pools along the way. The cattle fought to get tanked up and no one tried to thresh that out; it was up to each critter whether she was aggressive enough to get tanked up. A horseman amongst them would have scattered them in all directions.

They did not 'noon' because they were still in the narrowest place with nothing for the cattle to do but drift while the men ate, so Sut kept the leaders trailing him until almost two o'clock, then the mountains grudgingly pulled back and left a wide place of about two hundred acres, with good grass. It was too small for seventeen hundred herd, but it would do adequately for an hour or so.

Pete drew back allowing the cattle to spread out. He and Jack Dineen turned back to find Burt. They loosened saddle cinchas beneath several huge old trees and dug food out of saddlepockets and were sitting comfortably in cool tree-shade eating when Sut finally reached them.

The food was not much, it never was on a drive where there was no wagon along, but being able to drink cold spring water and wash off dust, then sit comfortably without having to move, was worth something.

It was while they were lying sprawled, or sitting propped and smoking, that Morgan appeared from among the trees and brush along the east slope. He rode up, swung off, cared for his animal then, as was customary with Morgan, strolled over without speaking, took a place in the shade and began to eat before finally dropping a few words.

"I think we got company up ahead somewhere."

Three sets of eyes drifted over and lingered on Morgan, who ate, swallowed, then looked up to continue.

"Barefoot horsetracks got to the top-out on the east side from back a ways, then went along the rim for a couple of miles. Maybe that was last night. It looked like they made a camp up there. Then they cut down off the rim on the west side. I didn't go down there but stayed on the rim."

The other men were still and motionless as they watched Morgan eat and swallow again before telling them the rest of it.

"Maybe two miles on, they come back up onto the rim like maybe they was expectin' someone to be followin' them, and set up there for a while, then went down off the south slope out where there's a big meadow . . . They might still be in that big meadow. I only saw it from high up and didn't go too close." Morg gazed straight at Burt

21

Sommers. "But they sure aren't leavin' this area."

Pete sucked his teeth and looked around the ground for a twig which would substitute as a toothpick. He said, "How many, Morg?"

"Maybe ten, maybe a couple more."

"Barefoot horses?"

"Yeh."

Pete found the suitable twig and thoughtfully went to work with it. "Barefoot horses," he mused aloud, looking solemn, "an' riders who stay to the rims, like someone is after 'em, and ridin' around and around in one area." Pete spat. "In'ians. Burt, back at Cutbank did you hear anything about tomahawks bein' off the reservation?"

Burt hadn't. "No."

Pete pitched away the frayed twig. "Well, it sure don't sound to me like hunters nor grubliners." He grunted back to re-settle thick shoulders against the rough bark of a tree and Sut had a comment to offer.

"Reservation jumpers sure as hell. You know what'll happen if they stay below us down in this damned canyon, and stampede the cattle back up through?"

They all knew; unless they had agile horses beneath them they would be ground to mincemeat, and even agile horses might not be able to prevent that.

Jack Dineen said nothing. He listened to the older men, and watched them. Usually, Sut and

22

Pete took everything in stride and made jokes about danger and hardship. They were not looking very good-naturedly philosophical now. Jack studied the rangeboss. "Burt, what kind of In'ians they got up here; you know?"

Morgan had finished eating now. He cut in before Burt could reply. "The way they got the In'ians reservationed, sometimes several bands maybe even from different tribes in one place . . . Anyway, it don't matter what kind they are."

Morgan's last sentence was absolutely correct. Jack may still have had a clinical interest but none of the other older men had. Burt went to work curling up another cigarette. He almost never smoked one right after another one. He lit up and gazed at Morgan. "We should have stayed on the main trail."

Morgan was a fatalistic man. "If they're out to kill drovers and steal their guns and horses and all, Burt, it wouldn't matter much, because our dust would draw those bastards like honey draws flies."

Pete Smith brushed ants off and sat up straighter. He lifted his hat, ran bent fingers through his thick hair, re-set the hat and sighed. "Can't go back. We wouldn't even get out of this canyon before dark . . . Hell, maybe they're pot-hunting Indians."

No one was willing to either accept that assessment nor agree aloud with it. Most of the grisly, gory tales of depredating Indians came not from big war parties, but from these little bloody-hand bands of stronghearts whose seething frustration drove them off the reservations full of a need for violence and exertion to get the poison out of their systems. Bloody-hands made ordinary Indians look like saints.

"That's three to one," said Sut, "an' us down in a darned canyon an' them maybe on the overlookin' rims, an' us with no idea when they'll hit us, and them sneakin' in closer."

"Or maybe run the cattle back over us," stated Pete. "Burt . . . ?"

The rangeboss had been thinking. They could not turn back, as Pete had said . . . They *could* turn back, but they would lose a lot of time and Mister Bright was anxious to see his new herd of up-bred quality bred cows down on the Florence Basin range. Also, even if they did turn back and those broncos were after some white hides, turning back would not save anyone.

Burt said, "Morgan and I'll ride point, Sut. You and Jack push 'em along. They likely won't try to climb the canyon walls so we won't need wing-riders . . . Pete, go up on the west rim and scout for us. Don't get too close to anything, and if you see riders, stay back and signal to us." Burt leaned to unwind up to his feet. "That stampedin' cattle is a two-way trail. If they want a fight . . ."

The men arose, dusted off and went after their saddle animals. Morgan stood back with Burt. When they were alone Morgan made a tart comment.

24

"They know we're down here, and barefoot horses get too tender to fork after a while. They're already in trouble up to their butts. You can't hang a man any higher for killing ten men than for killing one man, can you?"

They went to their horses to head up and around the spread-out cows. A few sucked back even though the riders were not that close, but the older, more seasoned cows simply stood like stone statues watching, to be certain the pair of horsemen would not turn toward them.

Burt said, "Bred-up redbacks or not, they'd run."

Morgan demonstrated his years at his trade. "Down in a canyon like this it never takes much." His dark gaze went to the rangeboss. "Looks like we got something we didn't figure on, Burt."

There was an easy answer to that but Burt refrained from giving it. Every cattle-drive that ever went down a trail ran into something no one had anticipated.

From the rear arose the hooting call of Jack Dineen and Sut Sutherland. The cows had trail-savvy by now; the ones nearest the shouting men began to turn obediently southward. A few were reluctant. Those would be the ones which had not got as much grass as the others. There was no dust because the meadow had been rather solidly grassed over, but looking back at it once the cattle were leaving showed devastation from so many cattle, even for that short length of time, that it would require a couple of years for the land to look natural again.

Burt and Morgan were well in the lead. Where the trail narrowed again, with canyon walls closing in, it was about three or four hundred feet wide. There were boulders in the narrower places the cattle had to be careful of, some of those rocks which had tumbled from the high, rough slopes, were half as large as a cow, and immovable. But there was no hurry, the animals dodged around them handily. Once, Morgan pointed to a big greyish snake side-winding his way frantically out of the trail, probably frightened by reverberations which snakes detected through their soft underbellies. Seventeen hundred head of walking cows moving across stony soil sent forth wave after wave of those reverberations.

They watched the big snake make it over to the side of the trail and start upwards, lost sight of him in some underbrush, and looked on down-country where more often than not visibility was limited by bends and abrupt turns.

The sun was past the westerly heights now, so there was no direct heat, but like all canyons where the air was usually still, heat lingered.

Burt watered his horse and leaned across the saddle looking back from the trail-side creek where he and Morgan had halted. The drive was coming along very well. He said, "We made good time today, Morg."

The lanky 'breed also looked back. "Yeah.

26

How many days we got down in here?"

"Three, maybe four, according to Cutler, the feller up in Cutbank who sold the cattle to Mister Bright. After that we're supposed to be able to see the north end of Florence Basin." As Burt finished speaking he turned to regard the man beside him. Morgan looked straight back.

"I hope they got somethin' with 'em besides jerky and sardines," he said, and gave Burt one of his rare smiles, this one more sardonic than humorous. "If they've been raidin' along the way they'd ought to have some decent white-man food, hadn't they?"

Burt ignored the look and the question. "They won't have a fire tonight, Morg."

"That's all right, we'll find the bastards."

As they swung back across leather Morgan held his tough smile, and as they reined away southward so that the on-coming critters could also take advantage of the trail-side creek, he said, "My paw told me when I was a button the way whitemen made it up here was to hit before they got hit. The ones that waited to be hit didn't make it . . . We got to find those bastards first, Burt."

The country was rugged, miles deep, up-ended and trackless. Burt had seen many miles of this kind of territory. As they slouched along watching ahead and on both sides he said, "Needles in a haystack, Morg."

The lanky breed shrugged wide, bony shoulders.

3

Toward Nightfall

Pete signalled in late afternoon, then dropped from sight, and for a while Burt worried about him but evidently Morgan didn't because as he and Burt rounded a smooth canyon wall with the drive a hundred yards behind, Morgan said, "Country opens out a little down yonder an' those westerly hillsides come down easy. Pete'll be showin' up directly."

He was correct.

A half-mile beyond where the canyon walls on their left tapered down toward a place where in eons past a vast river had worn away the stone, Pete Smith appeared on his tired horse, sweaty and working on a fresh cud of chewing tobacco.

He dismounted to wait for Burt and Morgan to approach, reached under to loosen the cincha, then stood hip-shot trailing his reins. He spat amber as the riders came on up, looked around and said, "I don't know much about In'ians, but these ones sure do leave odd marks. They know we're down here, but they've passed up half a dozen good ambushin' sites."

Morgan said, "Did you see 'em?"

Pete spat again and wagged his head. "No. But they came down off the rims the same way I did, and unless I'm wrong as hell they're on ahead a short distance." Pete considered his tired mount. "I don't think they knew I was above them on the rims."

Burt thought that was true enough. "If they're broncos, they'd have ambushed you, Pete."

Morgan swung off to rest his animal's back. While leaning upon the saddle he spoke his thoughts. "What kind of country is on ahead, Pete?"

"Pretty much open, Morg. Not bad country for bedding a herd. Open for a few miles, then those damned mountains close in again. We'd ought to bed down where there's plenty of room for a bed-ground . . . And make a dark camp on the west side. There's some trees over there." Pete faced Burt. "I think if I was a bronco and wanted shod horses and guns, I'd let a drive get this far down-canyon. Sounds will only carry straight up, down in here."

Burt nodded. "From up above how far could you see?"

"A hell of a distance," responded the bull-necked rangeman.

"How does it look?"

"About like what we been passing through, except that maybe tomorrow night or the day after — if we get down there far — there's a river." As he finished speaking Pete twisted to study the

29

darkening westerly sidehill where it trailed off on a southerly course, and finally ended completely where a series of grassy dips and rises eventually helped create the wide place where he had suggested they make their night-camp. "Burt, I'm no tracker. Hell, most of that kind of stuff was dyin' out when I first took to riding. And what I know about redskins you could put in your eye and never shed a tear." He faced the rangeboss and the listening 'breed rider again. "But — wouldn't broncos have had a scout hangin' back, especially if they thought someone might be trailin' after them?"

Burt and Pete were the same age. Morgan was older. Also, Morgan knew more about Indians. He answered Pete while Burt was considering what to say.

"Yeah. Especially if they're reservation jumpers. There'd be reservation police on the trail, or maybe soldiers. But hell, a good bunch of broncos would get into country like this and half the darned U.S. army wouldn't be able to find just maybe ten or twelve of 'em. If they kept moving."

Morgan looked steadily at Pete. So did Burt, who finally said, "What's on your mind?"

Pete brought forth two small objects from a shirt pocket and held them forth on his palm for the other two men to see. "I don't think it's In'ians. At least it's not *all* In'ians."

He was holding two brown-paper cigarette stubs on his palm.

After a moment of silence the rangeboss said, "Right now, I'm beginnin' to wish it *was* In'ians."

Morgan agreed. "Renegade whites. Maybe In'ians and renegade whites." He sighed and said "Hell," with a gust of feeling.

The cattle were coming, their occasional lowing growing louder. Burt turned to snug up his cincha and re-mount. He said, "You two head on down to block the trail below the next wide place. We'll bed down early today . . . Pete, is there water down yonder?"

Smith was twisting up into the saddle as he replied. "Yeah. Whatever else this damned country has, thank gawd for the creeks." He and Morgan walked their horses on down the trail, and Burt stepped over leather to follow them as far as the wide place Pete had described, and which he and the other two riders had been able to see part of, from back where they had conferred. Down there, Burt satisfied himself the canyon walls were steep and rugged enough to discourage any cut-backs, then went southward a half mile or so to sit over in canyon-shade and await the arrival of the cattle.

Bovine-like, as soon as the leaders found another wide place with grass, and no horsemen up ahead to bother them, they turned off the trail to the left and right.

Burt made a smoke, sat with one leg hooked around his saddle-swells, watched the animals fan out, and waited until he could see Jack and

31

Sut before killing his smoke, straightening in the saddle to ride back to them.

He was not enthusiastic about a night-time manhunt, but he believed as Morgan's father had believed — hit before you got hit. Even in country like this which was made to order for ambushes and hiding places. Even at night when what little moonlight might filter down would not help a hell of a lot.

He thought of Donald Bright down at the Antelope ranch jovially welcoming the people who would be arriving to lie over for his daughter's wedding, perfectly comfortable, without a real worry in his mind. Then Sut waved through thin dust and Burt forgot about the home-ranch, grassed-over open country, and the pleasure of people enjoying themselves, and rode toward Sut and Jack while making a thoughtful study of the surrounding slopes, stands of tall timber, and man-high dense thickets of underbrush. He was sure they were being watched from somewhere, maybe from close by along the westerly sidehill, or perhaps from the rims, but most probably from on down-country if, as Pete had said, the broncos had kept riding after they left the high places.

He had a bad feeling. Without anything to inspire it, he felt as though the broncos were just about finished with their game of cat and mouse. Whether they knew they too had been discovered was something to think about. If not, perhaps Morgan's notion might be worthwhile. If they had figured out that Pete had been upon the rims riding down their back-trail, then sure as hell they would set up an ambush tonight, and that thought was unpleasant as all hell.

Sut and Jack watched Burt coming toward them. Sut quietly said, "He's worried." Jack did not comment and when Burt reached them they sat their saddles as Burt began talking. He told them what he knew and what Morgan had suggested. He then said he favoured trying it and Sutherland frowned a little.

"We don't know the country and it'll be dark, Burt."

The youngest rider in the crew made a prescient remark. "Sut, even if we don't find them, and I'm not lookin' forward to it, maybe ten of them and only four of us, moving away from camp will be a lot healthier than sittin' in it — if they're going to hit us tonight."

Sut sat and frowned and did not find fault with what Jack had said, but he continued to look unhappy as the last of the herd rushed off the trail where the bulk of the drive had already spread out to greedily destroy the fragile grass as they had done at the nooning place.

Burt led his companions over to the west side and around the grass-cropping cattle to a rendezvous with Morgan and Pete. They found a decent-enough place to make camp and turned their horses loose with hobbles on, up-ended their saddles and un-slung their blanket-rolls, going through all the usual movements of trail-riders establishing a camp, while Burt said, "I remember an old buffler hunter telling me when I was a kid that riding through hostile country a man always had a ticklish feelin' between his shoulderblades."

Pete irreverently answered that. "That'd be the only place, Burt. My butt's too numb to tickle."

They were in among tall white pines, and their arrival had upset a balance of nature rangemen always upset, if not at night-camp then during the day. Birds flocking into the treetops to roost, scolded and complained and fled in all directions; as shadows thickened they were upset. They had to find other roosts for tonight and they had to do it soon, because if they were caught still in the air by darkness they were helpless. That agitated scolding did not last long. The birds fidgeted, finally flung upwards into the air and fled. Down below five men ignored that; they had troubles of their own. Even if they hadn't had they would have ignored that. All their lives they had been upsetting the routines of other creatures, not wilfully but out of necessity.

The cattle did not bed down until darkness began to fill the wide place in soft layers, coming down off the high slopes as the westering sun sank farther away. Usually, it turned cold in canyons almost immediately after the departure of daylight. It did not do that up where the men were making their camp. In fact, for whatever reason, this particular night there was a noticeable promise of lingering warmth.

4

After Nightfall

It was not, as Sut pointed out, unheard of for Indians to use tobacco, particularly if they had been reservationed near a settlement or a town. But, as he also pointed out, it was not customary either.

"Whisky," he said in conclusion, "yeah; they pick up that habit fast, but not smoking."

Morgan and Pete and Burt had already arrived at a conclusion which was pretty similar to Sut's observation and said nothing. Jack unfurled his blanketroll without commenting. He was not concerned whether they were being stalked by tobacco-smoking redskins, or abstaining Indians *and* tobacco-using white renegades. All Jack Dineen was concerned about was that he had never in his life been in a range fight or a trail fight, and there were enough butterflies behind his belt to fill a big bush.

They sat around waiting for darkness, saying very little, carbines lying upon their blankets, solemnly studying the country around the wide place where the cattle were finally beginning to grunt down into resting positions to chew their cuds.

Burt finally said, "The damned cattle. . . ."

Pete concurred with the rangeboss's unspoken thought. "We'll be safe as long as we stay out of the open. No matter which way they run, if those bastards figure to stampede them, if we stay up a slope or among the trees. . . ."

Sut pointed. "We can commence by crossing to the southerly end of the west slope — when it's plenty dark — then get a little height, just in case they got a fire, but even if they haven't we can commence walkin' on around . . . Morg?"

The lanky 'breed was sitting hunched, long, sinewy arms locked around upraised knees, staring intently at the far lifts and rises. "Yeah, maybe so, Sut."

Burt said, "Or we can get out there and lie flat among the horses. If that's what they're after."

They were quiet for a while, each man busy with his private thoughts. They were a hell of a distance from aid, or even from a place where they might ride for shelter in case their enemies put them to flight.

Jack hugged his carbine and was grateful for the increasing gloom so the older men would not notice his pallor or other little tell-tale signs of something very close to stark fear. In daylight, this would have been bad enough, but in the darkness. . . .

Morgan stirred a little. "Burt's right. The horses. If we walked our legs down to stumps lookin' for their camp, we'd likely pass the bastards in the dark, or walk right into 'em and get killed. They're good at this sort of thing. We sure as hell ain't. The horses'll draw 'em."

Jack Dineen spoke for the first time. "Morg, the damned horses are out there in behind the cattle. It's open country. If something happens and the cattle stampede back up the trail and we're lyin' out there. . . ."

Burt arose, slung the saddlegun in the crook of a bent arm and said, "It's dark enough."

Jack got no response from Morgan as the older men pushed up to their feet, but Jack Dineen had one more point to raise. "We only got five horses and five carbines."

Someone answered dryly from the gloom as the men started along behind Burt. "Five *shod* horses are better'n a hundred tender-footed un-shod ones, Jack, an' there's never been a renegade who wouldn't pick up a gun when he could."

Experienced hobbled horses could sometimes hop faster than a man could run. By the time they found their saddle-stock it was well away from the west-side camp-ground, out where at least some of the grass hadn't been trampled or fouled by cattle. Jack looked back, then forward. They were in the approximate middle of the big meadow. If they had to run for it, the east sidehills were about as close as the west ones. He decided that they could probably make it; stampeding cattle took a moment or two to get their legs collected under them. And that was the uppermost thought in Dineen's mind as they halted out there within view of the horses, and knelt close to one another, each man making his own quiet survey of what was around them.

Pete whispered to no one in particular. "I've heard it said a man can *smell* In'ians."

Sut softly snorted. "I've been aroun' 'em some. They don't smell any different than you'n I smell right now, Pete."

Burt was on one knee, leaning on his saddlegun when he irritably silenced the men. "They can *hear*," he growled, and after that admonition no one said a word. A few minutes later Morgan set an example for the others by lying flat down in the churned grass. Jack had decided he would emulate Morgan. The others also went down.

It was a dazzlingly brilliant star-shine night. The moon, if it was to arrive, had not as yet done so, but all that star-blaze was a fair substitute. A man could see around for quite a few yards.

The only sound was of horses cropping grass, which was always good to hear. Now and then an animal would hop in its hobbles, coming down with a solid sound. Otherwise, even the cattle were quiet, for a change, and the night began to wear along.

Pete chewed and the others did not dare roll and light smokes so they fidgeted. It was not a matter of patience; they were no different from other men in that respect; they had the patience for a long wait, but now they did not know where they were in relation to their familiar world, and although they knew they had enemies around, they did not know where they were nor when they might either stampede the cattle with gunfire, or rise up out of the night and try to kill them, with more gunfire, or even without it.

Burt eased over beside Sut and whispered. "I'm going up ahead on the far side of the horses. Pass the word around — stay here until I get back."

Sut did not respond, he frowned. The idea of separating did not appeal to him. It would not have appealed to Pete nor Morgan either. If a gunfight started it would not be in their favour not to know they might be trying to kill their own rangeboss.

But Burt slipped away. He went soundlessly in a steady, cautious advance up and around the indifferent horses and came down several hundred yards ahead of the other men, found a slight swale and went down into it, waited for a while trying to pick up sounds of men ahead somewhere, failed at that, paused to wipe off sweat — this was not his idea of a good way to meet an enemy either, in a strange place at night-time — then he crept up to the eastern rim of his swale, and thirty feet away saw a moving hump which was not the right size for either a horse or a cow, and did not move like a foraging bear.

He placed his carbine in the churned earth and trampled grass, reached carefully for his sixgun and raised it, bringing the gun carefully up even with his right cheek, and waited. The moving object sank from sight, becoming little more than a rounded shape against the ground. For a while it remained like that, then it raised up without a sound and began crawling directly toward the lip of the swale where Burt was waiting.

It was a man. He did not have a carbine and was using both hands palms-down on the ground as he crept along. He moved with flawless motion, as though this business of stalking was far from novel to him.

Burt made out the dilapidated old hat and the face beneath it, but darkness under the hatbrim made it impossible to determine much about the shape or shade of the face. The man's shoulders were narrow and sloping. Burt was unable to discern much more about the man, except that as he crawled steadily in the direction of the horses, he moved his head and occasionally halted, perhaps to listen, possibly to get re-oriented in the proper direction. One thing was clear to Burt Sommers, the on-coming individual had no idea he was being watched and was crawling directly toward an armed man who was perfectly willing to kill him.

Burt had some decisions to make, with which he had no difficulty. He had an advantage. That, more than anything else, might be in his favour. If he could cold-cock his adversary before the stranger had any idea he was about to be attacked, the meeting would be over in a moment. He could shoot the man right now — and perhaps cause seventeen hundred startled, sorry-

eyed cows to spring to their feet ready to run —
and — if they stampeded northward Burt would
not be able to get out of their way before they
went over the top of him.

He regripped the sixgun, sweaty palm notwithstanding, lowered his head by degrees so as
to remain undetected, and when he was finally
able to hear the softest and faintest sounds of
cloth rubbing against cloth, he had just his eyes
clear of the lip of land. His estimate was that the
crawling man was now about ten feet in front of
him; he would come to the lip of the swale in
about two minutes at the cautious rate he was
crawling.

Burt eased slightly and very carefully to his
right. He did not want to meet the man head-on,
he preferred being slightly to one side. Then the
man suddenly halted and hung motionless as
though he might have detected something ahead.
Burt froze in place with sweat running down his
forehead and nose, the gun poised to be either
fired or used as a club, and scarcely breathed. He
used this moment to wonder if there might not
be another one behind the on-coming man, or
perhaps three or four of them coming on an
angle in the same direction. His conclusion was
elemental. He had to brain his adversary swiftly
and efficiently — and as soundlessly as he could.

The man inched forward, peering toward the
swale. Burt sucked back down and pressed flat.
For a moment or two now he would be unable to
see the man. The alternative was to continue to

peer over the rim and be seen, himself.

The man reached the lip of the swale and did not hesitate to look around, which was both his misfortune and Burt's great good fortune. As the man started crawling down the side of the swale Burt rose up from the waist, and swung with his gunbarrel as though it were an axe.

At the very last moment the man detected swift movement and instinctively tried to twist away from it. He partially succeeded, the descending gunbarrel missed his head and came down with paralysing force upon his right shoulder. The man let go an out-gush of breath with a groan of pain in it. Burt was on top of him forcing the man's face into the earth to stifle further noise.

The man tensed all over and rose up under Burt, arching in desperation and pain. Burt tried again to hit his head but now it was sunk forward on the man's chest so all Burt did was strike his shoulders up near the neck, but he struck hard.

The man hung there on all fours supporting Burt, like a gun-shot bear, probably half knocked unconscious and half sick with pain. Burt cocked the gun and pushed it against the man's exposed neck, and forced his adversary flat down upon the earth. He groped, found the hip-holster, yanked out the sixgun and flung it aside.

The groggy man did little more than attempt an instinctive move with his right hand to prevent himself from being disarmed, but his right arm did not obey very well.

Burt slid aside, grabbed dirty, greasy cloth and one-handedly flung his adversary onto his back with starlight shining upon the man's face, fully exposed now because the man's hat was part way back up the slope of land where the initial attack had occurred.

The man was dirty, covered with dark stubble from ears to jawline, had dark, ferret-like eyes which seemed now not to quite focus but which ordinarily would have been venomous looking. He had a wide, lipless slit of a mouth and although he was about Burt's height, he was nothing but bone and sinew, the kind of individual who would be tireless.

Now, however, he was hurt, and with breath rattling in his throat he looked up at the man above him who was holding that clubbing six-gun, eyes reflecting moonlight in an opaque way.

Burt told the man not to make a sound, then sat back listening. If there were more of them out there, and he suspected there were, he could not hear them.

It seemed improbable that only one of ten or twelve renegades would crawl down here to steal five saddle animals. Burt flung back the man's filthy, greasy old coat. There were several short lengths of lead-rope tied around the renegade's middle. He *had* come to steal the horses, and his intention had been to lead away two or three of them. Burt stared downward. Since his prisoner did not have enough rope to lead all the horses away, then there *was* another one out here somewhere.

He rolled his prisoner onto his side, heard the man's teeth grind as his injured right shoulder was pushed into the ground under the man's own weight, then Burt chopped downward in a short, powerful overhand arc and the renegade flattened out. There was a thin tear in his scalp where the steel barrel had struck. It began to ooze blood as Burt rolled away and strained again to detect sounds of the other one.

All he heard was the dull, rhythmic pound of his own heart.

He started back toward the far side of the swale intending to get back to Pete, Jack, Sut and Morgan, when he heard one of the horses snort. The next instant all the horses began to shift in their hobbles, and Burt did not wait this time, he rolled up out of the swale and began hastening in a bent-over run toward the horses. Now, he knew where the other renegade was!

The man was among the frightened animals. Burt saw him moving. He seemed to be hatless but before Burt could verify this the man must have detected the different sound of booted feet because he suddenly dropped from sight among the horses, probably flattening on the ground.

Burt did the same, he dropped, hoping the diluted darkness and the fact that he was no longer moving would hide him from searching eyes.

The horses began edging away in little, forceful hops, moving uncertainly as though they were not certain in which direction to move to elude the powerful, gamy scent of a two-legged creature.

The horse thief raised his chest and shoulders off the ground, head high, eyes searching. Burt prayed he might be undetectible and did not move until the horse thief dropped down and silently began to roll back toward the swale, evidently unwilling, now that he thought he had been detected, to pursue his original intention of stealing the hobbled horses. He rolled and crawled with Burt watching, divining the man's course and intentions.

Finally, when the renegade stopped, cautiously reared up again, Burt pointed his sixgun and waited. But the man had not made him out, he dropped and began crawling again. When he went past, Burt turned on his belly like a snake and after three rapid movements was within launching range. He rose up and sprang, using both boot-heels as springs. The renegade heard something, raised up — and Burt hit him head-on, trying to club with his handgun, but this time it was different. As the renegade writhed he raised a stringy, dark right arm, Burt caught moonlight off wide steel, and frantically blocked the forcefully descending arm. The man's knife was at least a foot long, wide-bladed, with a wicked scooped section just behind the tapered point.

Burt fought to grab the knife-wrist. Just as furiously his adversary fought to prevent him from doing that. Burt tried to club at the man's face with his sixgun, and hit earth. His adversary was as lithe and supple as a green twig. He lacked Burt's power and strength but was capable of swift, snake-like lateral movement. He got the knife arm into the air again, and this time Burt took a chance, got far enough upright to have leverage, caught the knife-arm with his left hand, let go of his sixgun to grab a double grip using his right hand also, and they were locked like that when a lanky silhouette came up without a sound, grabbed the renegade's hair, wrenched the man straight back, and struck savagely at the man's throat with a balled up bony fist.

The renegade tried to scream, tried to suck air with his mouth agape, rolled up his eyes to stare at the fierce, swarthy countenance above, then gasped and continued to gasp as the strength went out of his knife-arm.

Burt tore the knife free and flung it backwards as hard as he could. He met Morgan's dark gaze as he rolled off the horse thief. Morgan pulled the renegade along the ground, rasping, gagging, trying to swallow without much success, and as Burt retrieved his sixgun and straightened around to watch, Morgan let go of the renegade, knelt, lifted out his Colt and cocked it.

The renegade's eyes bulged. He had both hands at his throat. Morgan said, "Get up you son of a bitch!"

The injured man got half way to his feet and almost fell. Burt grabbed hair and mercilessly yanked him fully upright. The horse thief was gagging again. Evidently that blow in the throat had done more damage than it had seemed to. Morgan came over with his sixgun holstered, took the horse thief by the shoulder, spun him and kicked, hard. The man stumbled in the direction of Jack, Pete and Sut. Morgan's fury was obvious; by daylight his face would have shocked the men he rode with. By starshine in partial darkness only Burt was able to make out some of the raw cruelty in it.

Morgan waited until they were well away from the horses as he punched and kicked his captive along, to turn and say, "Was there another one? This one's only got two ropes around his belly?"

Burt explained about the first one and Morgan wagged his head. "Good thing I didn't do what Sut told me — stay back there." He jutted his chin at the captive. "Damned 'breed," he said scornfully. "Burt, you just can't trust 'breed In'ians." Morgan's big teeth flashed in a broad smile. All the terrible fury was gone that fast. He was ready to revert, to make camp-jokes again.

But Burt never doubted as long as he lived that if Morgan had dared use his gun back there, had dared fire it, he would have killed that horse thief where the man had been lying.

Sut, Pete and Jack Dineen were on their feet as Morgan and Burt came out of the darkness with their prisoner. The man was still having trouble with his throat but he appeared now to be in less pain as he halted to gaze at the astonished rangeriders.

Morgan knew what his friends were thinking. He put it into words for them, partially with bitterness, partially because it was true.

"Damned 'breed!"

5

On The Hoof

They did not ask the renegade his name, they instead asked how many of his friends were out there, and when he told them there had been ten of them, Burt explained about the first one he had encountered and what the obvious purpose had been for both renegades to be slipping toward the horses. But that was no surprise so Sut fixed the prisoner with a steady gaze and said, "You got full-bloods along?"

The prisoner answered hoarsely. "Six."

"Off the reservation?"

"Yeah."

"How much raidin' you fellers done so far?"

The 'breed gently massaged his throat as an excuse to consider an answer before offering it. Morgan growled at the man. "You lyin' son of a bitch."

The 'breed considered Morgan for a long time before speaking again. He probably sensed that there was one man among the rangemen who would break his neck without a second thought. He probably guessed why too; 'breed's had a bad

50

reputation on the frontier and throughout stock country and the people who resented this most fiercely were the 'breeds who were not dishonest.

"We robbed a stage," the man finally said, still looking directly at Morgan. "That's about all. Tried to raid a ranch but didn't make it. There was a hell of a bunch of men there and some dogs brought them down to the corrals . . . We killed two of 'em and run for it."

"And," said Pete, "you got soldiers or reservation police on your backtrail sure as hell. Maybe a cowman-posse to boot."

The prisoner did not respond. He gently massaged his gullet, looked all the rangeriders over, his black eyes not as hostile as they were sly and rat-like.

Pete blew out a big breath, ignored the captive and looked at the rangeboss. He was about to speak when Burt addressed the captive.

"How bad do your friends need our horses?"

The prisoner answered frankly. "Bad. We can't even make our horses walk over soft grass no more. We got to get new horses."

Sut said, "Mister, you're done for."

The prisoner looked at Sutherland. "So are you," he said. "You won't get out of this canyon. Nobody right in the head would even go down through here with cattle."

Sut did not reply. He merely looked disgustedly at the captive and turned toward Burt. "Well, it's out in the open now. They know we know who they are and all the rest of it . . . You want my guess? They're not goin' to slink around in the dark any more."

Sut did not add the rest of it, because he did not have to. They were down in the canyon with timbered and overgrown slopes on both sides of them. They could be bushwhacked as easily as shooting fish in a rain barrel.

Jack Dineen, who had been sitting there listening without commenting, now said, "One of us could head down out of here tonight and fetch back some help."

The older men acted as though they had not heard that; there was no place that they knew of to secure help, short of Florence Basin, and that was still about three days on southward.

Morgan sat slumped, knees crossed, long arms draped over his knees, steadily watching the captive. Finally he said, "Who are the renegades?"

The captive, more afraid of the other 'breed than he was of the other rangeriders, answered promptly. "A feller named Tom Slade — me'n a couple other fellers. Four of us, six broncos . . . Mister, Tom'll let you go if you give us them shod horses. We'll give you five of ours. You can make it with them — they're tender but drivin' cattle is a lot easier'n runnin' for it."

Morgan continued to sit there, arms draped, lanky form loose and slouched, gazing at the other 'breed. "Give you horses," he said in a bitter, lethal tone of voice. "You son of bitch I

52

wouldn't give you the sweat off my brow if you was dyin' of thirst . . . I'll kill you . . . First chance I get." Morgan turned toward Burt. "You got an idea?"

Burt had one. "Yeah. I know you fellers are dog-tired; I am too, but if we wait until daylight to continue the drive, like he says, we're goin' to be sittin' ducks down in here . . . Get the drive on its feet and started on the trail — right now."

For a while the men sat in thought, then Pete agreed. "Dark or not they can't go nowhere but straight ahead." Then Pete did as most rangemen would have done under these circumstances, he made a loud groan and said, "Burt; Mister Bright's goin' to owe me for working overtime." He got to his feet, turned his back on the prisoner and considered the hushed night over where the horses were. "I apprenticed to a blacksmith back home. It's a good trade; you never have to go nowhere, there's a roof over your head, a cafe up the road." He looked down. Pete and Burt and Jack were waiting; they knew the kind of comment which was now due. "A rangeman is a body who ain't got the brains gawd gave a goose . . . Let's go."

Not even Burt urged Morgan to arise and join them. They went forth with bridles slung from their shoulders to fetch back the horses to be hobbled, and Sut was carrying in addition to his own bridle, the rig for Morgan.

Jack looked back twice, and each time Pete or

Sut growled at him to mind where he was walking and look up ahead for the horses.

The animals had moved from the place where that renegade got among them. They had hopped southward and a little westerly in the direction of the bedded cattle. It required a little time to locate them because, regardless of their feeling that only two horse thieves had been out there in the night, they also knew there remained eight more horse-hungry enemies somewhere in the darkness, and they were very careful as they hunted the animals.

They also took their time approaching. If the horses got spooked and made noise, if there was someone out here with a weapon . . . By the time they had crooned their way, had got the hobbles removed and were starting back, Jack had made up his mind what had happened back at the camp in the trees and hung back because he did not want to see it.

But Morgan was waiting for them facing toward the noises they were making, and he was smoking a cigarette inside his hat, perfectly calm. He did not look as though he had been in a struggle. In fact he smiled a little when he thanked Sut for fetching in his animal, and when his gaze crossed with the stare of Jack Dineen, Morgan waited a moment, then wickedly grinned, turned and set about rigging out his horse.

Jack looked around for the captive. There was no sign of him. He allowed Pete Smith to lead his horse up close by for saddling and started to make an enquiry and Pete growled at him. "We don't have all night, Jack. Get the saddle on that damned horse."

Burt too, blurted half an enquiry when Jack tried one. Burt said, "You ride with Sut. Morg and Pete will ride together. From here on we got to sort of watch out for one another's backs . . . Jack, just mind the herd. That's all. Just keep the cattle movin' down-country."

Dineen let it end there; at least he was not so dense he did not realize that he was being told as diplomatically as rangemen could be, that what had happened back in the pine-tree-camp during his absence when just Morgan and the other 'breed had been back there, was over and finished with. The men did not want to know the details and they were conveying the idea to him that he did not want to know them either.

They used up a full hour getting the cattle on their feet. They had to do this prudently because, despite the fact that the renegades would probably hear, and understand, what was occurring, if they had busted the cattle up out of their beds, they might have spooked and stampeded in the wrong direction.

The leaders trudged on down between the dark-rising canyon walls. Not happy about having their rest interrupted, but at least with grass in their bellies and several hours sleep behind them, not entirely reluctant either. Also, whether the rangemen understood it or not, by now the air coming up through the canyon had a strong water-scent to it.

Burt hung back half expecting the renegades to come after them, but if they were back there they were making no move to come close or to cause a stampede. Perhaps they were puzzled over the renewed drive in darkness as well as the loss of two of their numbers.

But that was not going to last. Burt realized that too. In fact, the renegades did not have to make the cattle run any more than they had to come swirling out of the darkness firing and screaming.

All they had to do was try and locate their missing friends, and simply trail the drive, keep trailing it until sunup, then, with good light to sight by, shoot those rangemen who could not escape from their canyon, like shooting crows off a fence.

Burt gave that considerable thought too. Except for the seventeen hundred redback cows he was confident he and his riders could survive this running fight simply by going up along the sidehills exactly as the renegades were doing. But he could not exclude the seventeen hundred damned cows — that was why they were in here in the first place; those cows were their professional responsibility and it was always a matter of pride with rangemen that they did not lose a single animal if it was at all possible not to.

He wanted to roll a smoke. Instead he dismounted at a little stream where the cattle had fairly well fouled it, found a decent place to drink, and got down on his prayer-bones. The water was very cold. For a while afterwards he remained at the side of the trail well concealed by the slope behind him, looking back and listening.

But there was nothing to be heard over the moving herd on down the canyon a mile or so, and if there was movement back yonder, it was invisible to him, so he swung a-straddle and went along.

None of them felt safe, exactly. True, it was difficult to shoot a man in the dark, especially if he was a moving target and the assassin could not get close, but right at this point those facts seemed damned feeble.

Jack told Sut he thought life was a very fragile thing, and Sut's response was dry, "So is the weather, Jack. So are horses an' cattle. Everythin' I know of can't count on much in this damned life, but maybe rocks, and I don't envy rocks at all."

The canyon widened a little from the bedground on southward, which helped some. Also, although the darkness lay in solid layers along the mountainsides and to some extent out across the trail, moonlight from above mitigated it enough for the cattle to be able to see a fair distance ahead, and they therefore kept plodding along, heads down and swinging, tails wagging, big, mildly distended bodies jostling one another.

Morgan rode as he commonly did, loose in the saddle and taciturn. Once or twice he stood in the stirrups to look around. The last time he did this, then eased back down Pete Smith put his finger on the one thing which would confound their stalking enemies more than anything else.

"They're not goin' to pot-shoot us in the night, Morg. It's not because of us — they don't give a damn one way or another about us. But if they start a run and blow us out of our saddles they're goin' to lose five shod horses in the stampede."

Morgan rode a while considering that, then evidently accepted it because he did not look back any more.

Finally he said, "This damned short cut," in a tone of bleak disgust.

Pete agreed, at least in part. "Yeah. Because Mister Bright wants to see his new herd a couple of days early. But those bastards would have found us even if we'd stayed on the regular trail. They'd have seen our dust for twenty miles." Pete spat amber and considered the cattle up ahead. "Only, they aren't supposed to be runnin' loose. That's what folks pay their tax money for — so's hired lawmen'll keep renegades and broncos where they belong . . . Did you kill that son of a bitch back yonder?"

Morg did as he had done earlier, he rode along a ways before speaking again.

"Naw. I wanted to. I sure should have."

"What did you do?"

"Tied him to a tree. If he's got good teeth he can chew through and get loose in a day or so."

"Jack's sure you cut his throat."

Morgan turned a sardonic grin upon his companion. "Let him think so."

Pete shrugged. He was perfectly agreeable. He said, "I got a hunch those bastards'll be after us come daylight. They could empty saddles then and see which way the horses run."

Morgan reached inside his shirt to vigorously scratch. "I wonder how far back those cowmen an' reservation police are. Or soldiers. Or whoever in hell is after these bastards."

Pete was laconic about that too. "Too far," he said, and yawned mightily.

The drag was keeping up, for a change, the main body of cattle were walking right along. At least it was cool in the night, making a very noticeable contrast to moving down the canyon-trail in daylight this time of year.

Burt remained back a half mile or more but as the night wore along it began to seem obvious that whatever their enemies were up to, they were not going to make an attack in the darkness from the rear, so after the drive had been under way for a couple of hours he picked up the gait a little, met Jack and Sut and rode along with them in silence, until the younger man said, "Burt, I still figure that if one of us rode ahead we could get some help," and Burt shook his head about that, then patiently said, "They won't all be behind us, Jack. In fact maybe none of 'em are back there. They'll be on ahead somewhere, figuring about where we'll be come sunrise."

The implication made Dineen worry even more, but he kept silent. Sut looked over at him, half in sympathy because at Jack's age Sut had had the hell scared out of him a few times too, and half in annoyance.

Cooler air came sweeping up the canyon from the south. The men untied their coats and buttoned them to the gullet. Ordinarily that cool air would mean dawn was coming, but down in a canyon it could simply be blowing up-country off a snowfield somewhere in the mountains, or maybe from a body of water.

6

The Unexpected

They covered about as much ground during the long night as they might have covered in a day-long drive, and that cool air was more noticeable along toward false dawn.

There was no wide place to hold the cattle, though, so they kept moving ahead. In fact the canyon walls pinched in closer down here than they had anywhere back yonder. Burt decided to have his riders back in the drag where they would at least have the protection of the miles-long strung out herd until daylight arrived. There was no need for a point-rider in the canyon since the cattle could only go in one direction.

After false dawn when the darkness returned briefly, the riders halted, dismounted in the cold early morning and ever-hopeful Jack Dinneen said, "If their horses are so tender-footed they might not have been able to keep up last night."

The older men looked at one another, Pete spat aside, and Burt spoke as though Jack had not said anything. "Unless those bastards are a couple of miles on down-country, ahead of the herd," he said, then hung fire for a moment and started over. "I figure they got a fair idea where we'll be come full daylight, and be settled in down there, waiting."

Pete said, "Some of 'em. Maybe most of 'em, but sure as hell they're back here too, on the slopes or maybe farther back."

Burt said, "Any way you look at it, Pete, we got to get out of the canyon, off the open trail. If they're on the sidehills back here . . ." Burt shrugged with clear meaning, and Morgan agreed with him.

"Get off this damned open trail before daylight," he exclaimed. "We're pure targets out here. Up yonder, we may still get it, but at least there's cover up there."

Burt said, "We don't split up," and turned to lead his horse toward the westerly slope where twisted rock-pines and thorny undergrowth as tall as a man filled most of the shale-rock openings. There was no way for them to go up in there leading horses and not make noise. In shale-rock they could not have been silent even without horses, but as they moved over in that direction they had the comfort of knowing they would at least have cover, not the best kind but a lot better than no cover at all.

It was warmer over in the darkness where the trees and underbrush stood. It was also darker. Both sides of the canyon were dark over where there was cover and lingering gloom. Those slopes rarely got any daylight but the west slope got the least once the sun had passed its overhead meridian.

The cattle plodded along because they were accustomed to doing it, and quite possibly because the water-scent was growing steadily stronger even though that river the cattle broker back at Cutbank had said the drive would not encounter until about the third or fourth day, had to be many miles ahead.

If the canyon remained blocked on both sides, then the cattle only really had two courses to follow, the one on ahead, or if they were stampeded, they might reverse their course and come charging back up the way they had been travelling, a deadly tide of hooves and hides and horns.

If the trail broadened down below, in the direction of the river, and if the sidehills became less forbidding and precipitous, then the cattle might fan out, whether they were running or not, in which case, providing there was anyone left to do it, the DB rangeman would have to waste a day or so finding all of them and bunching them back down in the canyon again.

In the view of Burt Sommers, it was like being between a rock and a hard place. Where he finally halted beyond the shale-rock with gnarled pine trees around, to make certain his riders were coming, he met Morgan's expressionless gaze and said, "Down in Fort Collins a man once wanted to sell me a pool hall."

Morgan's expression did not alter. "You should have bought it . . . Can you see ahead?"

Burt started forward as he replied. "Yeah. A hundred feet."

They continued, and they made less noise once they got away from the loose shale-rock but there were no game trails so Burt had to not only try to set a course but he also had to do it in the best possible way for walking men to move southward while leading horses.

Sunlight arrived. Not down in the canyon but up across the high, bristly and uneven rims on each side of the canyon. There was reflected brightness without any sun-brilliance in it, and without any appreciable warmth in it either.

Visibility was improved though, and its arrival caused a bad moment when a mountain lion came down the slope among the rock-pines peering intently southward where he had no doubt caught the full, redolent scent of many cattle, and being a carnivore, and belonging to that variety of carnivores who were always ravenous, he did not look northward in time. Burt saw him, caught the tawny movement in the shadows and made out the big cat's full eight-foot length before the cat suddenly picked up sounds behind him, froze with his back arching, and turned.

Burt could have shot him with his sixgun. They were close enough to make out the details of one another's bodies and shapes. Burt's horse picked up the scent and lunged backwards, almost bowling Morgan over. The 'breed cursed, struck Burt's horse in the rear with a fist, and that commotion decided the cougar on his best course of action. He spun on hind paws and went back up the steep sidehill as though it were absolutely flat ground. Within moments he was far above the horsemen and still moving in a tan-brown blur.

Morgan saw him, finally, but none of the men farther back knew what had caused the commotion up ahead. Neither Burt nor Morgan offered to explain. Burt dragged at his frightened horse, Morgan thumped it a few more times from the rear, and eventually the horse stepped out, but very warily. There was no animal horses feared more. There was no horse-killer which could give his prey as big a headstart and still overhaul him and bring him down with a powerful bite through the neck.

Horses feared bears and wolves, but they could when motivated by abject terror outrun a bear, and they could, in most instances, band together and fight off wolves, but they could not defeat a mountain lion.

Burt's animal did not settle down for a mile. Morgan gave him plenty of ground in case something else should frighten him and he should pull free, whirl and start back. That did not happen and after two-thirds of the second mile had been traversed Burt found a fold in the lower slope which ran back about a hundred yards where a spring had, over the millennia, washed down all the surrounding stone. Here all five of the DB riders had room to stand with their animals, and here, finally, Burt explained about the big cat. Here too, Sut suggested that one of them scout ahead in the wake of the cattle, and do it without being burdened by a horse.

Burt sent Morgan. The others allowed their animals to muzzle among the stones and crop what little grass grew in this hidden place. Burt then went back the way they had come on foot to settle low along the ground to watch for movement.

If there were renegades back there, they were much better at this sort of thing than were Burt and his riders. He did not detect a sound of men and horses back there, and he did not pick up any signs of movement.

He waited; there was no need for hurry. In this particular case hurry could be lethal. He knew they were somewhere close, either on ahead waiting in ambush, or farther back like jackals stealthily slipping along looking for an opportunity to get five shod horses.

He eventually turned back, got back into the area of the seepage-spring and met Morgan's steady gaze. "They back yonder?" Morgan asked. Burt shook his head. "Maybe one or two of them but if they are they're damned good at this sort of thing."

Morgan agreed with that. "I told you so last night. I didn't find anything either. The cattle are plodding along. I think what's kept them going is a smell of grass or water."

Jack Dineen raised a rigid arm and in a breathless way said, "Look!"

Across the canyon a man on horseback was discernible among some crooked pines. He was looking directly across the canyon in the direction of the place where the DB rangemen were holding their horses.

It was difficult to make out much more than that the man was on a horse; even the animal's colour was shadowed by the trees. He sat over there like a statue. Burt made a guess at the distance; it was far too great for a sixgun and probably too great for a carbine.

Pete said, "Sure as hell he's seen us."

No one questioned that as they stood staring. Sut finally faced the rangeboss. "He won't be alone. Burt, we're not in the best place if they're all over there." Sut craned around to gaze up the nearly perpendicular, overgrown brush slope at their backs. They could not go up there, which left a withdrawal either ahead where they had never been, or back the way they had come in search of cover.

He started to face Burt again, then abruptly whipped fully around to stare up the hill. In a crackling voice he said, "Run for it!"

The other men heard the noise before they looked up and saw the landslide starting to gather huge boulders as it gained downhill momentum. It spread, too, along the north and south slope. It had a considerable distance to come before it overwhelmed and completely covered the seepage-spring area where Burt and the other men were reaching for a stirrup and the saddlehorn.

Jack Dineen's suppleness put him in the saddle a moment or two ahead of his companions. He did not try to go back the way they had come, perhaps because of the treacherous shale-rock footing he knew lay in that direction. He spurred his startled horse out toward the open trail. Behind him Burt, Sut, Pete and Morgan followed Jack's example. As Jack reached the flat, unobstructed trail-area he reined northward. Behind him Burt was drawing his sixgun before he got down there. So was Morgan. Sut and Pete made no move to draw guns until they were out of the trees, and by then the roaring landslide drowned out every other sound.

When the gunshots erupted they sounded inconsequential against that other increasing rattle and roar. Whole trees were ripped up and rolled ahead and amid the spreading devastation.

Gunfire sounded scattered as the riders hung in the hooks and followed Jack, who was riding bent over his horse's neck. Burt looked backwards and upwards once. Some of the rocks hurtling toward the canyon's lowest spot were larger than a horse. They flew, left the ground and literally flew end over end.

Morgan was riding sideways using his carbine one-handedly. He knew sixguns would not reach although his companions had been using them.

He also knew a carbine being fired as he was firing his would be almost totally inaccurate, particularly from the back of a terrified, running horse, but Morgan's anger was up.

The slide continued to spread, but the horsemen were moving up the canyon faster than the widening tumult spread. They eventually got past the place where they had first decided to leave the canyon floor before dawn. Up that far the slide had almost exhausted itself. Back down where the little seepage-spring had been, however, there was an almost deafening thunder as tons of earth and greater tons of rocks reached the canyon floor, smashed together, broke into pieces, rattled over as far as the lower hill where that watching horseman had been, then began to accumulate in a high, loose earth — and rockfill blocking the trail completely for more than two hundred yards.

Burt hauled down his panting mount, turned it and looked back. Dust as thick as anything any of them had ever seen filled the canyon where the fill was. It spread both ways and reached up higher than the canyon walls.

The noise continued even though the full force of the landslide was diminishing. Up the slope on the west side where the slide had begun, there was a widening path of complete devastation; there was no longer a tree up there, nor a large boulder. Down where the seepage-spring had been there was absolutely no sign of that little arroyo.

The men swung off and stood looking back in awe. One man remained in the saddle but the older men ignored Dineen until Sut looked around, and gave a sudden grunting sound, then Pete, Morgan and Burt also turned.

Jack slid down the side of his horse, struck the ground without making an attempt to break his fall, and rolled half over onto his back.

He was dead. The older men saw the spreading claret stain on his shirt in back, and went up to kneel and ease him over. The bullet had hit Dineen high in the chest and only a very short space from his heart. Sut said, "I don't see how he managed."

Burt put Jack's hat over his face to keep out sunlight and dust.

7

Fight!

They were permitted an hour. During that time they took Jack over to the west slope where there was loose rock and shade, put his personal possessions into the saddlepockets on his saddle, and buried him beneath a cairn of boulders. They had no way to put up a marker so Pete and Sut pounded a torn pine limb into the ground at the head of the grave.

There had been scarcely a word said throughout. Jack had been younger than any of them. He had also been the best all-around stockman among them; that had never rankled with the older men. They had liked Jack, and right now as they were finishing the grave they were bitterly, coldly angry, so when the gunshot came and they heard lead bounce off nearby rock with an unnerving whine, they looked across the dust-chocked canyon to the west side perfectly willing to stop the backing and filling. As Burt said, "The cattle can't come back up this way if they run. That rock fill will stop them. I figure we got the time." He turned. Morgan and Sut were gently nodding while trying to see across the canyon where that gunshot had come from. The dust was too thick. It was also irritating to the eyes and throat. Pete cleared his pipes, spat and balanced the saddlegun in the bend of an arm. "They can't see us any better'n we can see them."

Burt started down away from the grave without a word. The others followed, leaving the horses back by the grave. That roiling dust made eyes water. It was an irritant in several ways but it was also, in another way, a godsend; it allowed the DB riders to get two-thirds of the way across the open trail before Burt motioned for the men to spread out, and while they were doing this someone fired at them from in among the dust-fogged trees and underbrush on the lower eastern sidehill. Morgan did not miss a stride. He fired his carbine from the hip. Whether he had actually found a target the others had no idea, but after he fired Burt said, "Hurry," and broke into a run.

Two more gunshots echoed up and down the canyon. Pete flinched; a bullet had come too close. He also changed course and finished his rush in a panting crouch.

They got to the first tier of underbrush, which was a variety of chaparral, or seemed to be; at least it had those little sharp spines chaparral had, and as the men began working their way through they got torn clothing and scratches, but if they realized this they gave no indication of it.

Burt halted beside a big bush to look for his companions. He had one brief glimpse of Morgan's recognizable lanky form, then it disappeared, and he did not see Sutherland nor Smith at all.

Up the slope where the dust was not as thick, Burt heard someone, or some*thing*, making a hurried retreat. He left the big bush to try and see up there, but pines cast a camouflaging series of interlocked shadows up there and he did not see the withdrawing individual.

Someone did though. From the left and roughly parallel to Burt a saddlegun's blast sent reverberating echoes bouncing up and down the canyon, and the noise of someone scrabbling in the shale-rock up the slope increased.

Burt went forward very carefully. He had no idea whether all the renegades were over here or not, but he surmised that more than one man was, and also guessed that the renegades had been scattered by the landslide, which would have accounted for the length of time it had taken them to find the DB riders over at the grave-site.

He did not think of the odds. There were now four DB men instead of five. He guessed that there were two less renegades, but that still left the odds at two to one, with the advantage, up until now at any rate, with the attacking broncos and their outlaw companions. Like his companions Burt was bleakly and coldly hostile and willing. The killing of Jack Dineen had completed

73

the feeling of indignation and had brought Sommers to the point where he would have taken the initiative if there had been several times as many renegades as there were.

By moving laterally he was able to utilize the underbrush and trees, but he saw nothing to shoot at and only twice did he hear anything and both times it was north of him, over where his companions had disappeared.

He was ducking under a low limb when someone on his right fired and chaparral leaves sprinkled over his head and shoulders. He dropped like a stone, heart beating in a drum-roll cadence, and did not move. He could not have crawled to cover before the hidden gunman shot him so he lay sprawled and motionless, waiting. It must have been a good simulation of a dead man because after a while he detected the skulking sound of someone approaching from below and to his right. There was faint sound of chaparral limbs whipping back after someone had passed along, but that was all for a while, until a sudden, fierce and thunderous exchange of gunfire to the north erupted, and after that the stalker did not make a sound. Burt guessed he had been distracted and was listening.

When the gunfire stopped as abruptly as it had begun, the man started forward again, but now he seemed to be hurrying, perhaps because he thought he had killed the DB rangeboss, wanted to strip the body of weapons and hasten over where that savage exchange had occurred.

Burt was on his face, twisted slightly to his right. His hat was askew, shielding part of his face. With one eye he watched for a shadow or a true sighting, and when he finally saw something close by, it was a pair of ragged buckskin trousers above a pair of moccasined feet. Beyond guessing the man about to lean and lift out his sixgun was an Indian, he could tell nothing; whether the man was large or small, fat or thin, with a gun cocked in his hand or not.

He did not breathe and made his body as limp as possible. He felt the hand fumbling at his holster, sucked a shallow breath of air inward, and whipped over, caught the reaching right hand with both of his hands, and wrenched as hard as he could. He caught one glimpse of a darkly bronzed face with aquiline features, a pair of wide-sprung black eyes, then the Indian was being hurled off-balance.

Burt released his grip as soon as the Indian struck the ground, uncoiled up off the ground and aimed a vicious kick as the Indian was also whipping up around to spring upwards. The boot-toe caught the bronco under the ribs in the soft parts of his middle. The Indian made a strangled outcry and sagged to the right. Burt was after him with another kick. This time he connected with an inflexible hip-bone, knocked the Indian off-balance and he fell to the right, twisting to look upwards as he fell, and instantly, with the suppleness of a snake, rolled out of kicking range.

Burt reached for his sixgun. The holster was empty. The Indian was coming up off the ground, but slowly and clumsily as though the pain in his belly prevented him from moving any faster.

He was not a young bronco. His face was lined, particularly around the eyes and down at the outer corners of his wide, nearly lipless mouth.

He was a muscular, supple man, scarred and tough and durable. Burt saw the sixgun in his waistband and the sheathed big fleshing knife on his right hip. He took two long steps, closed up and as the Indian pushed back to rear up, Burt struck him under the ear, grabbed away the sixgun, and was about to cock it when the Indian fell rather than jumped to his left, against Burt's legs. He was dazed but instinct warned him that he was going to be killed in a moment. Desperation made him do that. Burt staggered, nearly fell, then backed away and the Indian reached for his sheath-knife.

Burt cocked and aimed the old sixgun.

The Indian looked steadily upwards into Burt's face, did not take his hand off the knife-hilt but did not draw the knife either.

Burt said, "You son of a bitch," and sprang at the Indian. Now, finally, three seconds too late, the bronco wrenched out his big knife. At the same time Burt swung the gunbarrel in an overhand blow. The bronco's long plaited hair jerked as the gunbarrel came down across the Indian's skull, hard. The bronco dropped forward with his knife two-thirds out of its sheath.

Burt watched welling blood push upwards from the broken scalp through coarse black hair, moved back a step and stood gulping air staring at his vanquished attacker. He swore because he should have shot the Indian instead of clubbing him. This was not a fight among compassionate foemen; besides, he had nothing to tie his Indian with and he dared not leave the man behind him, injured though he was. Finally, he could not now shoot the man.

He wasted five minutes cutting strips from the greasy buckskin britches to securely tie the unconscious reservation-jumper, wrists lashed behind his back, ankles crossed and tied with several wraps and two hard knots, then he stood up again, found his own gun, holstered it and flung the bronco's old sixgun into the distant underbrush.

There was not a sound. The dust was beginning to dissipate back down across the open area of the canyon floor where the trail was, and sunshine lay upon the heights of the west slope, creeping steadily downward.

Burt's shirt front was soggy with salt-sweat. He pushed it off his face with a sleeve and thought of a drink of water as he stepped past the unconscious bronco heading over to his left where the cover was better, carbine trailing at his side.

Sut rose up out of the shadows on the north

side of a big bush and hissed. Burt turned, carbine rising, then stepped over into the same shadows and said, "Where are Pete and Morg?"

Sut pointed up the hill to their left. "I saw Morg cross among some trees up there, stalkin' someone. I been kneelin' down here waitin' in case he flushed one of them . . . Pete — I got no idea, but over yonder northward I think."

Burt turned to study the up-hill slope Sut had indicated and saw nothing. If Morgan was up there, he was being very cautious.

Sut said, "I heard someone shoot from back yonder where you came from a while back."

"Bronco," stated Burt, still ranging a probing glance uphill. "I knocked him over the head and left him tied."

Sut matter-of-factly said, "Why didn't you shoot the bastard?"

Burt did not have a very good answer to that. "Should have," he conceded, "but hit him over the head instead."

Sut did not pursue this topic. He said, "I figure there was maybe four of 'em over here. When we busted in among the bushes they commenced goin' back up the hill . . . Someone tangled with 'em northward a while back."

Burt nodded. He had heard all that gunfire too. He was still seeking a sign of Morgan up the hill. Finally he said, "Are you sure it was Morgan up there?"

Sut was sure. "Unless he's got a twin brother dressed just like him, I'm sure . . . An' I think he might be gettin' a little too far ahead."

Burt thought it over before speaking again. "Let's go up there."

"What about Pete down here?"

Burt did not reply, he arose with the saddle-gun in his hand looking for the safest, most protected way to ascend the overgrown, stony slope. He was not a general of troops, he had never done anything like this before. All he knew at this moment was that Morgan might be going into trouble. Pete — wherever he was — would have to do whatever was required of him to stay alive, just like the rest of them had to do.

Sut followed. They zigzagged uphill on a southerly angle utilizing every bush and tree and dark shadow. They also had to stop several times for breath. The slope was steeper than it appeared to be, and neither Burt nor Sut were mountain-climbers. Like all professional rangemen, they did nothing like this under normal conditions unless they could do it on a horse.

The last time they halted to pant for breath Sut gestured. "To the left from here. See that big old split-top pine? That's where I last saw Morg. Movin' around toward the south. From the way he was actin' I figured he had someone in sight."

Burt's thirst was beginning to occupy more of his thoughts as he squeezed off more sweat and began sashaying in and out among the trees and underbrush again.

There was less undergrowth up this high, and more pines, but they were more often than not separated by several yards of unprotected country. Except for the faint filter of tan dust at this elevation, and the shadows cast earthward by treetops, each time Burt stepped ahead for the next protective tree he and Sut were exposed.

But nothing happened. No one fired at them.

They came to an erosion wash which looked to be at least fifty or sixty feet deep, and down there the underbrush was so thick and interwoven they could not see the ground, but they could hear water trickling over rocks beneath the brush.

For a while they utilized a pair of arrow-erect pine trees while they looked down there. There were no birds, which would have had a significance to an Indian or a professional hunter, but to cowboys, at least for a while, that did not mean a thing.

Sut made a soft sound and when Burt turned Sutherland pointed eastward on down the deep gully. Burt turned and watched again. Eventually, he detected the faintest of movement among the chaparral tops. Something was moving through down there, very slowly and very cautiously. It was more likely to be an animal than a man, but Burt knelt, snugged up his carbine, cocked it and waited.

Very slowly a tall, rawboned silhouette began to rise upwards, hat askew, shirt torn, the skin beneath many shades lighter than the bronzed, aquiline set of features which eventually showed as the man turned his head very slowly looking in all directions. Even from the distance Sut and Burt could see the expression of puzzlement and disgust on Morgan's face.

Burt eased down the carbine, let the hammer back down and without raising his voice said, "Morg; up here. Where did you last see him?"

Morgan stood stone-still until he placed Burt, then he gestured ahead on down the arroyo but did not answer aloud.

Burt studied the entire onward down-hill slope of the wash and saw nothing, not even movement, so he spoke again without raising his voice. "He's hiding in there sure as hell. We'll go along from up here, parallel to you. Flush the bastard out and we'll finish it."

Morgan's lanky form disappeared back down beneath the tall, thick underbrush, and a minute later a man's gruff, frightened voice came out of the brush about five yards on down the hill from Morgan.

"I quit! Don't shoot, I quit!"

Burt called down there. "Stand up where we can see you!"

The cornered man was frightened but not foolish. "You pass your word you won't shoot?"

Burt's answer was curt. "Stand up, you son of a bitch, or we *will* shoot!"

When the man stood up with little more than his head and shoulders visible, Morgan came up on the renegade's left no more than fifty feet, and cocked his carbine. The renegade bleated.

"I surrendered for Chris'sake! My gun's on

the ground, I ain't armed, I surrender!"

Burt and Sut held their breath. Morg was staring straight at the renegade. Burt called to Morgan. "Herd him on down the draw. We'll meet you down there."

Burt and Sut had another bad five seconds before Morgan moved to comply. During those five seconds the renegade's life had not been worth a plugged *centavo*, but once Morgan moved to drive the prisoner ahead, Burt and Sut sighed, arose and turned back the way they had come to reach the bottom of the slope in time to meet Morgan and the captive.

8

The Lariat Rope

Burt had a long drink of water where the creek which flowed beneath the underbrush of Morgan's arroyo came out into open country among grey rocks. He and Sut had a short wait before Morgan appeared with his prisoner. They killed that time by speculating about the whereabouts of Pete Smith. There had not been a sound or a gunshot for fifteen or twenty minutes. Whatever was left of the renegades, Burt thought it was fair to assume that they had withdrawn farther back up the mountainside.

Morgan grounded his carbine and leaned upon it. Because the saddlegun was short and Morg was tall, he had to bend far over. His black eyes were fixed upon the sweat-drenched prisoner with an awesome intensity. It was clear to Burt and Sut that Morgan would kill the captive if he could get the smallest excuse to do so.

Burt had misgivings so he sent Sut with Morgan back over where the grave was, which was where they had left the horses, then he went northward in search of Pete.

The silence was deep and enduring, most of the dust had settled and until the next rain arrived this entire canyon area would have layers of dust over everything, the trees, underbrush, grass, rocks, the blocked-trail on both sides of the high, thick stone and debris blockage which cut completely across the canyon's bottom.

It was on the men too, streaked by sweat. They looked thoroughly disreputable. As Burt eased back and forth looking for Pete he occasionally paused to scratch. Maybe it was the dust, maybe it was the perspiration. Most probably it was a combination of both.

He came through underbrush within sight of a half-acre clearing. There were brass cartridge cases out there reflecting sunlight. This, he thought, was about as far north as any of them had gone. Pete had to be around here somewhere, unless he had gone back across the canyon, which did not seem likely, or unless he had, like Morgan, gone after a renegade.

He hadn't. Burt found him sitting beside a lichen-scabby boulder, carbine leaning at his side, with a bloody bandage around his upper left arm. Pete was chewing and did not appear startled when Burt crossed the little clearing toward him. He spat, squinted and said, "You get any?"

Burt told him about Morgan's captive and Pete spat again and said, "Captive, hell," and leaned to use his right arm to hoist himself upright. "I wouldn't take a captive." He got partially to his feet, looked critically up the slope and said,

"There was two of 'em up yonder. We had us a regular little war until one of 'em shot me in the arm . . . Are they gone?"

Burt thought so. "Yeah, but except for Morg's prisoner and a buck In'ian I cracked over the head, they'll still be around . . . Can you walk?"

Pete picked up his carbine with his right hand. "Sure I can walk. I was a little light-headed until I got the thing tied off, but I'm all right now." To prove it, Pete stood up, waited a moment, then turned to head back down toward the open area at the bottom of the canyon.

Burt watched him. Pete was *not* all right. He walked flat-footedly the way a man would walk who was carrying a hundred pound sack of grain on his shoulder. His shirt-sleeve was in rags, the shreds of it, and the left side of his trousers, were blood-soaked. When he halted to rest beside a tree Burt asked if the arm was broken and Pete shook his head. "No. It was a carbine slug and went right on through. Tore out some meat is all, but it bled like hell before I got it tied off . . . Anyone else get hurt?"

They resumed their slow walk as Burt replied. "No."

Pete suddenly halted and turned. "You hit one over the head?"

Burt knew from the cowboy's expression that he did not approve of this any more than he approved of Morgan not shooting his prisoner.

As they walked along, out into the open and on across toward the west slope, he explained about his Indian attacker, making it sound as though it would have been indecent to shoot the Indian, which it had been, but when he had finished Pete Smith growled a valid point of disapproval. "Burt, the more bastards we leave alive in this world, the more grief we store up for other folks."

Morgan and Sut were over there. The horses had strayed a little to search for grass, of which there was precious little, and had been brought back. Morgan's prisoner was sitting on the ground moving only his eyes. When he saw Pete and the blood on his clothing, the prisoner kept anything from showing on his face but his eyes brightened. He and his companions knew how many drovers there were — five — and this man at least now knew that one was buried beneath the nearby cairn, and now here was another one who had been wounded and had lost a lot of blood.

Morgan shook his head at Pete. "Did you make 'em pay for that?"

Pete sank tiredly down. "No. They had timber to hide behind. But I ran 'em off . . . You got any water?"

Morgan went after a canteen.

Sut and Burt stood regarding the prisoner. He was a gaunt-looking individual who would normally be stockily built. He probably was not as old as the lines in his face indicated, but there was no mistaking the malevolence in his soul because it was reflected in his cruel, lipless mouth and in his unwavering pale eyes.

He was a man any of the rangemen would have disliked on first sight. He looked evil even when he was controlling his expression so as not to antagonize the men around him. He said, "All we needed was the horses. We didn't mean you boys no harm."

Pete twisted from his seat on the ground and said, "You lyin' son of a bitch. We caught one of you fellers back a few miles and left him tied to a tree. He told us what you been doing."

The renegade shifted his glance away from Pete's face. "We had to do *something*," he said defensively. "There was some fellers after us. Damned deputy marshal and a couple of reservation policemen, and a township constable where we stopped a stage to get a little money and some food." The prisoner looked around again. Morgan had returned and was standing there listening, holding a canteen. The prisoner pointedly did not look in Morgan's direction as he went on speaking.

"All we wanted was the horses. We'd have left ours for you. It wasn't us started the fight."

Morgan moved, handed the canteen to Pete and faced the sitting man. "What would you call it when you fired on us when we run down out of here to get away from that landslide?"

"Well; you was makin' off with the horses," answered the prisoner, looking sideways at Morgan, then looking away. "I seen you bustin' away from over here through the dust. The first feller

87

was riding a sorrel horse. I yelled back to the others."

Sut said, "Then you fired."

The prisoner looked over at Sut. "To stop you before you run out of the country. We got some bad-off animals, an' we got the law behind us. What would you have done?"

Sut did not answer. They were all gazing at the prisoner. Jack had been the first to charge out into open country, and he had been riding a sorrel horse. As the silence dragged out, their prisoner sensed something, guessed he had said something he should not have said.

Pete turned finally to readjusting his bloody bandage. Sut looked from the prisoner to Burt, and Morgan said, "Burt, let's tie this one to a tree too."

They ordered the prisoner to stand, which he did, ragged, gaunt, filthy, his opaque pale eyes moving among his captors. Morgan went after a lariat and when he returned they herded the prisoner up through loose rock where several bull-pines stood. There, Burt and Sut bound the captive, buckled the man's shellbelt around his ankles, and as they straightened up, the man's eyes began to widen. To tie him to a tree as they had done to their other prisoner they would only have had to require him to face a tree so they could loop rope around him and the tree.

When a man was hanged they buckled his legs together and tied his arms behind his back.

He stood staring, losing colour by the second.

Finally, as Sut moved to catch the slipknot end of the lariat Morgan was preparing to cast over a pine limb, he said, "Listen; you can't do this. I didn't hurt no one. Mostly I hid down in that draw when you fellers come chargin' over at us. Listen fellers; I can help you get Tom Slade. He's our head man. They got rewards on Tom from Montana to Arizona."

From back where Pete was trickling water from the canteen over his hot upper left arm came a bitter growl. "Get it over with."

Morgan flung the rope and Sut caught it. Neither of them looked at the captive while Sut pulled out some slack. Burt made a smoke and when the renegade opened his mouth to plea, shoved the smoke in then flicked a match as he said, "That's how much time you got, mister."

The renegade spat out the cigarette, sweat was streaming off him. He stared from bulging eyes at the rangeboss. "I didn't do nothin' to you fellers. All I wanted was to get a shod horse under me. The law's after us, for nothing — for helpin' some In'ians bust out of the reservation. They live bad up there, don't have enough to eat." Finally, the prisoner faced Morgan. "I could have shot you," he exclaimed in an unsteady voice. "When you was up the slope before you come down into the draw I could've shot —."

"You didn't see me up there," stated Morgan in a bitter voice. "I didn't cross the topout, I angled around toward the draw."

The man was quaking now. "Mister," he said to Burt. "We buried a cache of money we got off a stagecoach up near the entrance to this canyon. I'll take you up there and dig it up for you. There's five thousand in greenbacks. If you boys split it up you'd —."

Morgan gently took up the slack and turned toward Burt. "Lend a hand."

Sut crossed over too. They hauled and strained. The renegade jack-knifed his body, he screamed until there was no air left to use for that purpose, he twisted one way, then back the other way. He made deep-down sounds and continued to arch his body, to wrench up his knees and kick outward. He was not as heavy as any of the men straining to hold him aloft with dug-in bootheels and bulging muscles, but because of the way he strained and jerked, pitching and straining as he swung wildly, pendulum-like, the men on the hangrope had all they could handle to keep his feet off the ground.

Finally, they got twice around the tree and Burt tied off the turk's-head end of Morgan's lariat, then the three of them stood back gulping air.

The strangling man's violent struggle lessened. Morgan said, "We evened it up for Jack."

Sut turned away, heading back down where Pete was waiting. "Leave him up there," he muttered.

Morgan started forward too, but scowling. "Like hell. That's my only lariat."

9

Beyond

They did not know how many enemies they had left. Two had been killed, two had been brained, but the brained men would not stay down indefinitely and while they might not be able to do much, they would still be armed and out there.

Jack was buried and Pete had a useless left arm. As they left the grisly place where they'd had to pile stones atop a second corpse, Burt leading, picking his way far up the slope so they would be able to go around the landslide-blockage and come down south of it, Morgan told Sut that it was going to require more than just a miracle for any of them to see Florence Basin again, and Sut had simply grunted because he did not like high places, and where they were navigating the slope was where the landslide had unsettled the entire area. Each time Sut's horse staggered or slipped, Sut's jaw-muscles bulged and he swore at the horse.

They were two hours getting up and around the blockage and for most of that time they were in plain view. Burt was of the opinion that while they would be unable to conceal their presence and obvious destination from watchers upon the opposite side of the canyon, they would be far beyond even carbine range, and unless the renegades had already started up and around the blockage, they would be unable to stay parallel with the DB riders, and he bitterly smiled at the thought of those renegades trying to urge horses which were already sore-footed, up around the landslide area where there was nothing but sharp rock.

It was mid-afternoon before they could get down off the sidehill again, down where the trees and underbrush had not been disturbed, and the first man out of his saddle when they found a little willow-shades creek, was Sut. He watered his animal, filled himself up, got aside so the others could do the same and stood gazing back up where they had circled around like four spiders on a nearly vertical wall. He shook his head and fished around for his makings.

They rested for fifteen minutes. Morgan, who had been leading along the spare horse with Jack Dineen's outfit on it, left his companions to prowl up ahead, around a bend to see what was up there.

When he returned he said there was not a single cow in sight, but there was abundant sign that they had passed this way, then he also said, "There's a place about a mile down where we could cross to the east side and be in tree-shade all the way . . . We got to get over there."

Pete was kneeling at the creek trickling cold water over his swelling, bad-looking wounded arm. "Unless they kept up with us," he told Morgan, and got a growl about that.

"Naw' even if they don't go huntin' that feller we lynched or the tomahawk Burt brained, they couldn't make as good time on sore-footed horses."

No one argued with Morgan. Burt in fact was not even thinking of how they would cross the canyon without being seen and shot at. He was thinking of seventeen hundred head of up-graded, bred redback cows. If that landslide hadn't stampeded them he would eat his saddle. And if there had been a stampede, then there would be some dead cattle too; the canyon was too narrow for so many cattle to go blindly charging at full speed, without having a few stumblers which the rest of the herd would have ground underfoot. The question was: How many?

Pete arose and went to lean on his horse while he fished around inside his saddlebags for something to eat. Morgan had plenty of jerky, they had cold water, and Jack was not going to need the flat little tins of sardines Burt dug out and handed to Pete.

The wounded man sat in shade, ate, drank water, afterwards brought forth his plug with one hand, managed the entire operation that way and returned the plug to a pocket after cheeking a cud. He looked pale and he was profusely sweating. He had trouble mounting and dismounting, but when Burt said they would rest here a little longer Pete growled.

"What the hell for? We could get across the canyon, and by gawd this time it'd be us sets up a damned ambush."

Morgan smiled and when Pete led his horse beside a boulder to mount Morgan watched in case Pete needed assistance. He didn't, but it was not his usual smooth mount. As Burt headed down around the lower sidehill among the pines Morgan got beside Pete and asked how he felt.

Pete was a physically powerful man, bull-necked and rough. He answered frankly. "It only really hurts when the damned horse stumbles or something like that, otherwise it just sort of aches in a dull way. I guess if the bone'd got busted it be different." He used his right hand to lift the left one out of his shirt front, then waggled the fingers of the wounded arm. "Everything works," he said, and shoved the arm back inside his shirt. "What I'd sure admire to have is a drink of whisky."

They had none.

When Burt found the narrow place with the jutting trees on both sides he paused to intently study the eastern sidehill, lifted out his sixgun and started across. Nothing happened. All four of them got across, even Morgan who was leading Jack Dineen's riderless horse and was bringing up the rear.

There was sunshine up near the topout on this side of the canyon and there had been none on the west side since mid day. But they did not expect to go up that high as Burt turned southward again. What he particularly desired was a sighting of hairy redbacks. He was not seeking an ambushing site, he wanted to know about those cattle, which were his responsibility.

But he did not see a single cow. He picked up the smell of cattle, saw their tracks and encountered broken bushes and small trees where they had gone past, but there was not a cow as far as he could see.

When he twisted to speak to Sut who was directly behind him he said, "Well hell, if there are no dead ones so far, maybe there won't be any."

Sut did not reply because he had reservations about that, as any professional rangeman would have had. There would be casualties; there had never in the world been a stampede of so many cattle through a narrow place like this, without there being casualties.

But Sut was not as worried about the drive as he was about renegades perhaps getting parallel with them, but a few hundred yards up the slope, so he rode along peering up there.

As before, though, after the underbrush thinned out at the lower elevations there was nothing else for men to hide behind but trees, and a man on a horse could not hide very well, behind a tree.

It was Pete, replacing the canteen by its strap

around his saddlehorn who finally said, "Burt, those bastards are behind us sure as hell. They wouldn't have been able to be ahead. I'm useless in a fight now anyway, so I'll just sort of drift back and watch for 'em."

The rangeboss got annoyed. "You won't do any such a damned thing. If they're behind us, they'll be a fair distance back there, and we'll keep moving until we find a decent place to stop."

Nothing more was said for a solid hour, by which time the sun up above was no longer showing down the sidehill, it only showed up along the final hundred or so yards of the topmost rim.

They did not find another place to halt until much later, by which time it was apparent that wherever the renegades were they were not close enough to use guns, and, as Morgan thought, they probably were not close enough to see the DB riders.

He was probably correct. By the time they stopped, with early evening coming down through the canyon, the country was widening out again, but now the wide places seemed more frequent and the grass down here was stronger.

Sut, however, left his companions when they stopped to rest the horses, and climbed up the sidehill because, as he explained, this might be their last chance to see if anyone was back there.

The place where they stopped had several cold-water pools fed by an uphill spring the men did not see. Pete got down low and put his aching left arm completely under the water and when Burt came along after the livestock had been cared for, Pete looking up almost smiling. "Hell of a relief," he announced. "I been thinking — if folks had ice handy it had ought to help out in something like this."

Burt knelt to study the water. It looked as clear as glass. Still, as he said, soaking like that might allay the ache but if the water was contaminated. . . .

Pete shook his head. "I've drunk water a lot worse than this an' it never killed me."

They let the horses crop grass, of which there was an abundance, and Sut rummaged everyone's saddlebags for a meal which he parcelled out after returning from his up-hill scout. He had seen nothing and he had heard nothing. When he wagged his head about this Morgan passed it off with a shrewd observation.

"Like we figured back yonder — tender-footed horses wouldn't make it through all that jumbled, busted rock, unless they were pushed to do it, and even then they'd favour and pick their way." He also said, "But they got all night to catch us," and went over to a pool for a drink before returning to complete his statement. "We'll be waiting. There's bound to be a place on ahead for bushwhacking."

They rode away from the cold-water pools with enough daylight to last for another couple of hours, even down in their canyon, and Burt who was up ahead, found more of those wide

97

places. He also found a crippled cow. She was alone and barely able to hobble. If Jack had been along he would have diagnosed her problem correctly as a thrown stifle.

Burt guessed that was what it was from watching how she moved when she saw the four riders coming toward her up the grassy place where she had been standing. Each time she moved he could see her hip joint bulge.

Morgan wordlessly took down the lariat he had salvaged back yonder, shook out a loop, and with Sut backing him up, moved ahead. The cow would have run past if she had been able to. Morgan roped her, took his dallies, and while she fought and sat back, and Pete called encouragement, Burt and Sut ran in close and upset her. Then they pulled her sprung leg far forward, and while she whistled for breath and tried to kick, Burt dropped all his weight downward. Sut heard the ball grate back into the socket.

Burt remained atop the hip joint while Sut worked his way forward to sit upon her head as he worked Morg's last rope loose. She could not arise without getting her head up first, and now finally, able to fill her lungs again, she did not make an effort until Burt was satisfied and called forward. Sut got off and moved away. Burt was getting off when the lunging cow expedited his departure. The men withdrew and allowed the old girl plenty of time to test her leg. It supported her; they did not crowd her so she walked painfully but at least with all four legs bearing weight, out of the glade to the trail, turned southward with the gamy scent of cattle in her face, and kept walking.

Sut sighed. "Damned cows," he said, "damned renegades, damned canyon . . . I'll buy into that pool hall down in Fort Colling with you, Burt."

Pete, having been relegated to the position of spectator, had been examining the glade they were in. Up the north slope, which was a gradual incline, there was no underbrush at all and very few trees until the higher elevations were reached. He pointed these things out, then turned to jut his jaw Indian fashion to indicate a little grassy spur-canyon over along the south-west border. "If they come, they got to come across the glade," he told his companions. "It's too danged steep for them to slip around above us yonder. I figure it's about as good a place as we can find."

They allowed Pete to lead the way. The ride required about fifteen minutes, and when they reached the spur canyon they discovered that farther back, past the funnel mouth, it widened until back where the mountain rose nearly vertically at its back, thick with pine and fir trees, there was roughly two or three acres. There was no water, but they off-saddled back in there, hobbled the horses, dumped their equipment down at the narrow place so the horses could not go past, and took a little while to get comfortable.

There was still daylight. Not much but enough, Burt thought, to last until he could scout southward looking for the cattle, but on foot it would take too long, he had used his horse hard enough for one day, and climbing the mountain at their back to see southward would use up all the remaining daylight, so he abandoned the notion.

Pete got comfortable. His arm was badly swollen. It was also discoloured but he told them except for the dull ache, there was scarcely any pain, and even the ache was less since the soaking back a few miles.

Sut scouted for a creek, found one, brought back two full canteens and left one with Pete. The horses were thirsty so shortly before the last light Burt and Morgan took them to the creek. While they were over there Burt said, "I got a feeling they'll keep coming, Morg."

The lanky 'breed was watching their horses guzzle water. "Maybe not. Sure as hell they run head on into a hornet's nest. Unless they saw us cross the glade and come up in here, they won't know where to find us. We got no fire and the country's full of pockets." Morgan looked out across the dimming glade. "I don't much like the idea of not settlin' up with them, Burt . . . For Jack, and all the rest of it."

For a while the rangeboss was silent. He was tired, they were all tired and gaunted-up and dirty. They hadn't eaten very well either. He appreciated how Morg felt, but going back to hunt for the renegades would cause even more hardship, and it might not be very productive. By now the renegades knew they had met their match, superior numbers notwithstanding. They had lost two men, and had two more badly beaten. Their saddle animals were unable to keep up the chase with any kind of haste, and actually, as Burt told Morgan as they turned to lead the tanked-up horses back, it was up to someone else to catch those men, to punish them, he and Morg and the others had a more direct responsibility — get the bred cows down to DB range in Florence Basin.

Burt's reasoning was fine, and many men would not have faulted it, they simply would not have sympathized with it. Men like Morgan — and Sut and also Pete — were doggedly resentful and bitterly antagonistic toward those renegades. The cattle were going nowhere; up ahead, since the country was obviously widening out and opening up as it progressed toward Florence Basin, the herd would find plenty of places to laze time and graze. It might take an additional day or so to backtrack in a manhunt, but Morgan was perfectly willing to postpone a few meals and some sleep. As he and Burt walked back leading the horses Burt knew Sut would be willing too — and Pete, except that Pete's body was not going to be equal to the demands his mind would make on it, and his companions would realize that.

Burt — was not willing.

When they got back with the horses and hunkered in fragrant late dusk, heard wolves out eastward somewhere, perhaps moving along the scent of the cattle, Burt reiterated his objection and no one agreed nor disagreed with it for a long time.

Eventually Pete said, "The horses aren't up to it. Not do that, then come back, pick up the cattle and keep on drivin' down to the basin. No grain, not enough grass. . . ."

Sut smoked and sat cross-legged like an Indian, looked at Morgan and shrugged.

Morgan glanced at Burt, then stared at the soft earth in front of where he was sitting. "That's the difference," he mumbled "between redskins and whiteskins. Redskins'd find those sons of bitches and leave 'em lyin' for the buzzards to find."

Sut sighed and yawned, then smiled at unsmiling Morg. "Redskins didn't have seventeen hundred head of cattle they'd hired out to look after."

Morgan finished his smoke and went after his blanketroll. He did not say another word.

10

A New Day

Burt sat up for a while, less to keep watch than because he had things to sort through in his mind. So far he thought they were on schedule, although the cattle were more responsible for this than their drovers were. That landslide had sent the herd southward in a rush; the men were still far behind them because they had spent a day man-hunting.

By tomorrow, perhaps in the afternoon, they should find the herd, perhaps down by that river the livestock broker back at Cutbank had mentioned. If the cattle were down that far, then according to Burt's calculations they should be almost out of the mountains in the direction of Florence Basin.

For no particular reason he thought of his employer and the festivities at the home-place where the marriage had either taken place or would shortly take place. About that he said an earthy, coarse word and put those thoughts out of his mind as he felt around for his tobacco sack.

The night was warm, even in that tucked-away

place; there were stars up through the clearings by the thousands. Somewhere there was also a band of renegades; they had been hurt and humiliated by less than half their number of angry rangemen. Ordinarily Burt supposed they would not abandon their vengeance trail, but with horses incapable of keeping up the chase, and with fear in the men's minds about the lawmen who were on their trail, it was quite possible that the renegades would give it up, turn off eastward and try to make up the lost time, and mileage, they had squandered in their effort to get the shod DB horses. If they did indeed give up and turn away, Burt was perfectly willing to have it like that, but he too, except for his first responsibility, would not have been averse to going after those treacherous bushwhackers.

He thought of Jack. He remembered when Dineen had first hired on, how he and the older riders had thought Jack would be just another young rangeman. He remembered how savvy Jack was about cattle, how he had never complained, had always pulled his weight, and how everyone had not only liked Jack, but had respected him as well.

What a hell of a way to end it, under a pile of damned rocks up in a canyon where not ten men would pass the grave in that many years, without even a decent marker.

Burt stubbed out the smoke. Someday, when he had the time, he'd like to return and put up a decent stone.

He never would. No one ever would. They would intend to, though, and they would never forget Jack Dineen. Perhaps that was the best shrine anyway, to be remembered fondly for as long as a man's contemporaries lived.

Morgan raised his head and quietly said, "You aren't goin' to be worth a damn tomorrow."

Burt smiled.

"Bed down," stated the lanky man, "and I'll spell you off . . . Those bastards couldn't find us anyway. Not even redskins can read sign in the dark."

Burt said, "Stay in your blankets. I'll bed down in a few minutes."

Morgan remained propped up, like a turtle with just his head high. "You thinkin' about the kid?"

"Yeah, partly."

"If I get a chance someday I'll come back and stick up a decent marker . . . Anyway, he went over the divide doin' what he did best an' what he wanted to do." Morgan yawned and scratched his awry hair and scalp. "I think we lost 'em, Burt."

The rangeboss nodded. "Yeah."

From farther off a disgruntled voice hoarsely said, "Shut up an' go to sleep!"

Burt went to his blankets and piled in. Morgan sank back down and heaved a noisy sigh. Overhead a high moon soared majestically on its unending orbit, and except for some nearby rustling where varmints were out foraging, along with the occasional 'thump' of a hobbled horse bobbing in search of better feed, the night ran on toward a chilly dawn.

When they rolled out, wordlessly packed their blankets and looked at one another, someone asked Pete how he was doing and got back a rough answer.

"Fine. Just fine. My whole damned shoulder and arm ache, my butt's sprouting calluses, I smell like a billy-goat and itch — but just fine."

Sut laughed in relief as Burt and Morgan went after the rested and fully fed horses. It was cold, but even so Pete went over to the watercourse and hung his feverish arm in the water — and gasped because it was like being in a snowbank the water was so cold.

They took the horse to him and pretended not to watch as he found a boulder and used it to mount from, then Morgan led off through the trees on around the haunch of hillside beyond which lay the trail.

But they did not go out there. Whether the renegades were no longer after their shod horses or not, prudence did not get as many people hurt as recklessness did. They followed around through the trees until Morgan was satisfied they had put enough country behind them, along with twists, bends and peaks, then he looked back and Burt nodded, so Morg worked free of the cold slope and got out into the canyon bottom where there was abundant sign of cattle having recently passed along this way.

They found a dead cow, entrails strung out for a hundred feet, while the sun was nearing its meridian, otherwise they did not find additional casualties. But they got a fright as the sun peeped over the eastward rim — Sut and Pete abruptly squawked and yanked around to head for the cover of the eastward sidehill. Burt and Morgan twisted, going for their weapons. They had heard nothing but obviously Pete and Sut had.

A ponderous and slow-moving big body emerged from the shadows of the back-trail and Morgan raised his sixgun. It was that cow they had worked on yesterday. She must have been walking most of the night to get down this far. She saw the riders and halted dead-still, watching. Morgan let go a rattling breath, leathered his weapon and joined Burt in also turning off the trail.

They waited patiently for the old girl to limp past. She kept an eye cocked in their direction every step of the way, ready for flight if any of them moved, even though she could not possibly have run. They gave her plenty of time and Pete was embarrassed as he said, "Darn fool animal."

They followed the limping critter without getting close enough to worry her, the sun finally breasted the peaks and moved directly overhead spilling warmth down into the canyon. The men shed their coats and as Burt looked at them he wagged his head. They had torn shirts, filthy trousers, badly scuffed boots, unshaven faces,

Pete had caked dark blood on his clothing and had not regained his colour, and they were about as dirty as men could be who had been on the ground without time to sluice off for several days.

Morgan saw the head-wag and said, "We'll be drawin' flies directly." Then he grinned, something he did not do often. "You reckon we'd be welcome at the wedding?"

Sut also grinned. "I'd rather attend one as a guest, even smellin' like an old goat, than be a party to one."

Pete had a comment to make about that which indicated that he might not be suffering too much. "I wouldn't mind — if she was a rich cowman's only child . . . I'd lord it over you fellers. I'd work your butts raw — but by gawd I'd never make you take no damned short cut with a bunch of cattle."

The old sore cow up ahead halted in the middle of the trail, lifted her head, tested the air for a moment, then lustily bawled. Afterwards, she limped along a little faster. She had picked up the warm blood scent of other critters.

The sun was moving away from the canyon bottom as Morgan rounded a long-spending curve where a mountainside began to suck back making the canyon straighten slightly in the saddle. He pointed and said, "River, by golly."

They came around that long bend and halted. Not only did they have a wide, shallow, glistening watercourse on ahead, but down here on both sides of the river the hills were retreating and where they had been was a large grassy place perhaps eight or nine hundred acres in size — and it was full of complacent cattle, grazing quietly, or lying up close where there was shade, eyes half closed, chewing their cuds.

Burt looped his reins, hooked a leg around the horn and fished forth his makings. As he rolled a smoke he said, "I wonder how cold that water is?"

Sut answered immediately. "I don't give a damn. I'm goin' to waller in it like an old sow — and wash my britches an' shirt too."

Morgan glanced far back. "You'll look funny as hell scamperin' for dear life naked as a jaybird if those bastards come along."

Sut was scornful of that possibility. "Pee on 'em. If they'd been back there they'd have tried something by now."

Burt agreed with that. "Yeah. But if they do — this time let's not use ropes, let's drown the sons of bitches."

The cattle looked up, stonily watched as the four riders and their horses came down into the big meadow, but made no move to run or bunch or shy clear.

There were many places to camp. The DB men chose a site on the west side of the meadow, which was tucked back in a fold of hills where it would be possible to keep a wary vigil of the back-trail and the eastern slopes, which had almost no trees upon them, less underbrush, but

109

lots of clump-grass which grew almost stirrup-high.

If the renegades came, no matter how they did it, they were going to have to come into clear view if they attempted to reach the river-meadow. But by now the DB riders were relegating that possibility, and that peril, to the back of their minds.

Pete went down to the river to bathe his arm. Sut went along and did exactly as he had said, left his filthy clothing on the soggy grass, kept his hat on though, and went out into the river. The water was barely above his knees so he had to lie down to become fully immersed. He had a small chunk of brown lye-soap along and threshed and puffed as he scrubbed. The other man watched, laughed, and called encouragement.

They freed the horses, in hobbles, draped booted carbines from bush-limbs, unrolled their blankets so they would absorb day-long heat and thus be warm after nightfall when they climbed in, and rounded up what food they had left, which was enough for another two or three meals, providing they made it last, which they would do because that was how men in their situation always did, then Morgan found a warm place, stretched out full length, hung his hat down over his face, crossed both hands across his chest and slept. Bathing could wait.

Burt did as Sut had done, stripped bare except for boots and hat, scrubbed his clothing, stretched it across warm rocks, then had a smoke while hunkering in the afternoon warmth. Down here where the mountains had become rolling, thick hills, with much lower topouts, the sun still warmly shone.

He studied the cattle, could not possibly make a count but made a fair estimate, saw the limping old girl contentedly cropping grass among her friends again, looked for more cripples, found about a dozen, all of which were on their feet, indicating that whatever injuries had befallen them in the stampede they had not been too serious. Cattle would lie down and remain down if they were seriously injured; like people, they had their share of hypochondriacs; some old girls would lie down in abject pity for themselves over nothing more injurious than a barked shinbone.

The sun continued to sweep away westward, the heat lingered, Burt's clothing dried, except for the pockets, and as he considered dressing, Sut came back up from the grassy riverside in his two-thirds dry clothing to find a place to lie back as Morgan had done and nap with his hat over his face.

Pete was rewrapping his bandage, scrubbed clean now and dried in the sunlight. His arm was about half again its normal size, much of the caked blood had been soaked out of his clothing, but like the rest of them, his shirt was a rag, he looked completely disreputable but moderately clean for a change, and cracked lips along with beard-stubble made Pete look more villainous than a genuine renegade. But he was feeling better, which he proved as he sank down near Sut and said, "Burt, it's damned hard to respect a naked rangeboss, especially if he ain't any more impressive than you are without your britches," and that was when the mud-dauber struck. Burt leaned to lift his britches off the stone where a number of hornets had congregated, and one of them flew upwards in a rage and stung Burt in the left cheek.

The rangeboss sprang away whipping his britches around at the hornets, cursing and moving like a clumsy dancer. Sut lifted his hat, partially raised up and looked. So did Pete. Morgan came down out of the tall grass and halted in astonishment to watch.

Burt finally reached back. "Damned hornet," he exclaimed, feeling for the stinger.

Morgan resumed walking. As he passed the rangeboss he primly said, "Serves you right, flauntin' yourself like that."

Burt extracted the stinger, got dressed, and went forward toward the other men, watching every step because those stinging little yellow-striped varmints did not live in high nests like wasps, they lived in holes in the ground, they were absolutely fearless, and would boil out of their underground nests when they felt the reverberation of footfalls coming their way.

The men shared a meagre meal, enjoyed a little tobacco afterwards, and when Burt suggested walking out a ways to look at the herd, Pete declined. He wanted to sleep.

It was not possible to get too close, nor was there sufficient sidehill cover for concealment, so they made a big sashay over against the eastern sidehill, well clear of the nearest cattle, and made their assessment. Sut said it was a damned miracle they hadn't lost better than a dozen head and Morgan concurred. He also said, "We can cross the river come daylight, but there are some limpies out there — we'll have to poke along for their sake . . . How much farther, Burt?"

The rangeboss had no idea but he hazarded a guess while scratching the itching place where the muddauber had stung him. "Maybe another day. Maybe we'll see Florence Basin by late afternoon."

They stood a while in the dwindling late-day pleasant warmth until Sut said, "Y'know, it come to me just now: A man could file a claim on this country up here. It's not too far to drive 'em out in the autumn. A man could set up his buildings up this here sidehill facing the river. . . ."

Burt and Morgan turned a little to study the broad river side meadow from a fresh viewpoint, and eventually Burt nodded his head. "It's a good idea, Sut. You wouldn't be ridin' into town every Saturday night, but it's a good idea."

They started back, the nearest critters left off being warily watchful, went back to eating or hunting up soft places to bed down, and out across the wide river some fat trout leapt to feed off skimming bugs.

Pete was sleeping like a log when they got back. They considered him, Morgan placed one of Jack Dineen's blankets over the blanket Pete had pulled up, then the three of them sank down for their final smoke of the day as Burt ranged a long look all along the slopes and ridges, and up the canyon as far as it was possible to see, but it was already dark back up there.

He said, "They gave it up."

Morgan and Sut did not require elaboration. Morgan still had rankling thoughts though. "Lousy bastards," he said quietly. "I hope to hell those lawmen who are after them take the lot of them back belly-down across their saddles . . . I would."

Pete stirred, muttered and resumed sleeping. The other men sat a while longer then also rolled in.

The cattle were bedded, the fish had stopped jumping, there was no moon for a long time, an hour later in fact this night, but that incredible rash of high stars glittering like diamond chips overhead in their curving vast vault of heaven cast enough light earthward to prevent full darkness from existing.

11

Angry Men

The cattle were hesitant, not because the river was cold but because they had no idea when they would wade out past the shallows, sink to their bellies and have to swim for it. But that did not happen, the river, whatever its name was — if it had one — was especially wide in this area of the big meadow, and therefore it was also no more than a couple, perhaps three, feet deep, at its deepest point.

When the leaders climbed out upon the far shore behind Sut, who was riding point, the rest of the herd was already half-way across and no longer very hesitant.

It was a cold morning. Every morning was cold in the high-plateau country, except for a few weeks near the end of July and through August, but at least the sun arrived sooner now than it had back up the canyon, and that helped.

Pete was feeling much better. He still had his swollen, discoloured arm folded into his shirt-front but he told Burt he thought some of the swelling had gone out of it, and he attributed

115

that to the frequent soakings in cold water. Burt had no idea whether this was indeed the case but for Pete's sake was perfectly willing to believe it was.

From here on, the trail was much wider. In fact before noon Pete had to peel off from riding stirrup with Burt and go over along the west side. There were more divergent canyons down through here, all invitingly grassed-over and warm.

Burt kept the drag moving. Now, it consisted mostly of either sore-footed critters or ones which had injuries from the stampede. He did not push the animals, and therefore fell steadily farther back. Not, he told himself, that this mattered since they would all come together again when they halted later in the day, or when they left the diminishing hills and emerged into Florence Basin.

The morning warmed up, the sky was flawlessly azure, the bleak, harsh mountain pass was behind them, and as unique that it was that they had only found one dead cow Burt was perfectly willing to accept this benefice from God, or whoever it was that watched out for trail drovers.

He was gaunt, had no idea how ragged and disreputable he looked, and as he rode slightly to one side in the saddle favouring the red, mildly swollen place where the mud-dauber had stung him, with a warm, beautiful world on all sides, his four-legged responsibilities plodding steadily along ahead, he had his faith in range-bossing restored.

There were bends in the trail, not as abrupt as they had been miles back, but in most cases more prolonged so that by midday, with his slow drag, Burt had lost sight of the mass of the drive up ahead. He rode casually, hat tipped down against sunlight-reflection, conscious of the strong, gamy scent of cattle, which had always been rather pleasant to him, and the thin dust which had begun to arise shortly after the dew had been burned off.

He saw a pair of bald eagles leave a huge, unkempt nest atop a dead fir tree, taller than any of the living firs around it, and watched them soar and circle. They probably had nestlings up there and the herd's passing had upset them, but not very much because they did not leave the area nor even soar very high.

Burt had a smoke and angled toward a muddied creek on the east side of the trail to water his horse. He would have enjoyed water too, but not after the way the drive up ahead had fouled the creek. But the horse did not mind. Each time he swallowed his ears jerked.

Burt stood beside the animal, cigarette drooping, considering the opposite slopes where they seemed to roll endlessly westward, increasing in size as they went off in that direction, becoming more brushy, timbered and rugged, and when the horse partially lifted its head, lips closed with water dripping, while it looked intently back to its left and up the grassy sidehill, he paid no attention. And that was a mistake.

A nearly scarlet bluejay with his topknot raised in alarm flung away overhead making his raucous cry. Burt looked around and upwards, otherwise he would not have fared very well. As his head turned he saw the way his horse was motionlessly staring, and the very next moment the brittle voice hit him between the shoulder-blades.

"Don't move! Not one inch!"

Burt moved, he dropped like a stone, rolled beneath the startled horse, and the man back in the tall clump-grass fired too hastily, but he accomplished something — the horse shied violently and whirled, heading down toward the drive with his head high, stirrups flapping, reins swinging and jerking, raising dust in his belly-down race.

Burt drew as he rolled toward the nearest tall grass, fired twice as rapidly as he could, and either upset his invisible adversary or hit him, although he did not think he had been that lucky, but in any case there was no second gunshot from back up in the grass, as Burt crawled deeper into the sheltering grass and halted on his belly, heart thumping.

He had been sure they were not still coming. He would have bet his wages on it.

Someone yelled in a startled-furious tone farther back and Burt twisted, half-expecting to be fired at from across the canyon, but evidently the man who had yelled was not westward, it was the acoustics of the canyon that made it sound that way, he was northward, and somewhere above, up through the grass. He fired with a carbine and that flat, waspish sound had come from in front of Burt and to his left. The bullet struck ten feet out in the trail. All it accomplished was to frighten the limping cows and make them break over into an ungainly and painfully shambling trot. It also scuffed a small geyser of dust.

Burt burrowed ahead to get farther from open country in the direction of the man who had first fired at him. He was breathing fast, as though he had been running. There was no time to speculate, but if there had been he would not have considered his position as being anything but bad.

The gunmen up ahead somewhere, and to his left, seemed either uncertain where Burt was, or unwilling to disclose their own positions by firing, but in any event there was nothing left now to indicate that there had been gunfire but some diminishing echoes, and Burt took frantic advantage of this interlude to crawl to his right, praying that the tall grass would not weave sufficiently overhead to give away his approximate location.

Time moved along, Burt crawled, hampered somewhat by the sixgun in his fist but willing to overlook that and several other inconveniences to get out of sixgun-range as quickly as possible.

If they had to use carbines to nail him, they would probably have to either stand upright or at least get up onto their knees to shoulder and aim, and if they did that, although he did not have his carbine, the horse had left with it, he still had the sixgun, and out of range for it or not, it would certainly upset an exposed gunman. Or he at least hoped very much that it would.

But there was no additional gunfire and once, when he lifted his head inches above the tall grass to peer around, there was not a man in sight.

With growing hope he began to angle back down toward the canyon floor. Sooner or later his companions were either going to miss him or find his riderless horse and start back-tracking.

It was sooner rather than later. He heard them coming in a rush when he was no more than a couple of hundred feet from the trail, and increased his downhill crawl, and when he knew they would be able to see him, he took a long chance and sprang upright out of the shielding grass, flagged frantically with his old hat, gesturing for them not to go ahead.

Morgan saw him, hauled back with an outflung arm to halt the other men, then Morgan, with good instincts, left the saddle on the fly. Sut did the same but Pete reined his animal over closer to the slope before he dismounted.

Burt met them near the base of the hill and sank down upon one knee while gesturing for them to do the same. Then he explained what had happened. Sut squinted up the grassy sidehill. Morgan scowled blackly and sucked back his lips into a flat, uncompromising line.

Pete looked worried, or anxious. He alone could appreciate the real danger of being shot at, and hit.

Sut said, "There's nothin' movin' up there."

Morgan spat dust, let go a long breath and considered the rangeboss. "All right. They dang near killed you. Now let's get this over with. I'll pack you double an' we'll make a run for it northward up the canyon. Then we'll head up there on foot and try'n drive those bastards down here for Sut and Pete to thin out."

Sut scowled and pondered. So did Pete, but Burt was willing so he agreed with Morgan and as he and Morg arose to go back down to the horses, Burt said, "They got three ways to go to miss you, but if they come south. . . ."

Pete understood. "We'll nail 'em."

Morgan caught his horse out in plain sight and led him over for Burt to step up behind the cattle. Morgan was mad enough to take a chance, but there was activity up the slope through the grass.

When he and Burt were ready the horse, sensing something, kept fidgeting, so Burt had to grab a handhold in the back of Morgan's belt. It was a good thing he did because Morgan had in mind going up the canyon so fast they would be poor targets. He gigged the horse, hard, it was already anticipating something, and gave a tremendous bound forward and lit down running. Burt's grip on Morgan held the 'breed rangeman flat back against his cantle.

It only took moments to get a half-mile up the trail. By then they were out of even saddlegun range. But Morgan did not slacken the run for another hundred or so yards, and he only did it then because the only tree-growth on the east side of the canyon appeared in sight. He reined over into the trees, waited for Burt to step down, then dragged out his Winchester as he also dismounted.

He offered the carbine to Burt but the range-boss wagged his head, stood a moment plugging fresh loads into his handgun, then reared back to look up the mountainside. There was a little underbrush back up the canyon this far, but not enough to make Burt feel safe. He and Morgan exchanged a look, there was no need for words.

Morgan sat down, shed his spurs, arose with the saddlegun in his hand, picked out the best way to climb the slope and struck out.

Burt followed, but spending much less time than Morg was spending looking up there, from bush to tree, and from tree to bush.

It was puzzling where the gunmen had gone. It bothered Burt more than it bothered Morgan. He was after targets, the whys and wherefores did not enter his mind. Morgan loved to hunt. Not necessarily two-legged creatures, but the four-legged varieties he had been hunting since boyhood were just as wily and clever at eluding detection, and were far better camouflaged for it, than the two-legged critters he was after now.

He halted a couple of hundred yards up the

sidehill to catch his breath, to stand pressed close to a warped pine tree and study the area. Burt was looking back downwards. Morgan grunted and when Burt faced ahead the 'breed pointed with a rigid arm to a dim but discernible trail through the grass where someone's passage had broken grass-stalks southward. It was a fairly wide trail and it was the only one around.

Burt said, "They didn't come back."

Morgan nodded. "On horseback, maybe four of 'em. That's about what's left of the bastards. They rode along the rim. How's come you didn't see them?"

Burt coloured a little. "Because I wasn't lookin' up here."

Morgan accepted this. He really was not very interested in how the gunmen had got past Burt anyway. He was far more interested in what seemed obvious — the gunmen were still down through the grassy country on the sidehill where it either tapered down in a southerly way, or to the west, over where they had fired at Burt.

While Morgan tried to decide which way to go Burt pointed to the tall-grass trail. "We can maybe get across without being seen, then get down on all fours on that trail and follow it."

Morgan did not hesitate, although if they had to follow the trail its full distance to the place where the gunmen had seen Burt and had tried to catch him, would be more than a mile of crawling.

Morgan was accustomed to inconvenience,

bruises and hardship. They all were; that's what their lives had consisted of since childhood.

They crouched far over and loped to the trail, dropped flat upon trampled tall grass over there and started crawling.

12

Pursuit

Burt eventually halted Morgan. What troubled him more now than ever was the absence of their attackers. He and Morgan had not been fired upon when they made their dash up the canyon, and after the initial attack down near the canyon's floor, there had been no further sign of his enemies.

Morgan listened impatiently, then gestured ahead. "They got to be up there somewhere. Look around, there are no tracks comin' back."

Morgan wanted to push ahead but Burt sat there a few moments longer trying to guess what their enemies were up to. Eventually though, when Morgan remonstrated, they crawled onward. Morgan's feeling was that the attackers were probably sliding down the grassy slope toward Pete and Sut. He wanted to catch them from the rear.

Morgan was a good sagebrush tactician. Most lifelong hunters were. Once, he halted to swear under his breath because his knee had come into solid contact with a partially buried stone. After that, he crawled more like a crab than a man in order to favour the injured knee. Also, he slackened off a little and watched more closely where he was crawling.

The rim was not very wide, perhaps two hundred feet at its widest points, and there was nothing up there but tall grass gently waving with itinerant little breezes which were so soft the crawling men did not feel them. On both sides, where the rim sloped away, was more of that tufted tall grass. There was no brush nor trees on the west side but on the east side at the sidehill's lower environs there was considerable undergrowth and scattered stands of trees, most of which were pines, but here and there stood a shaggy old cottonwood, and from this Burt guessed there was water down there, probably one of those little springtime piddling creeks.

But what he looked for he did not find; a trail where horsemen had gone eastward. Morgan had to be correct, wherever they were, it had to be southward somewhere although what puzzled Burt was that while the attackers could do as he and his companions were doing — hide in the tall grass — there should have been a view of saddlestock up ahead somewhere, and there wasn't.

Morgan abruptly halted, sat back on his haunches with his head above the grass, and for a long time did not move. Burt got up beside him and also raised up very cautiously because according to his estimate, as well as the way the land was beginning to slope downward, they had to be roughly in the area above Sut and Pete.

Burt sighed and pointed. "Trail. They cut down the east side and rode along just under the topout."

Morgan grunted about that. He wanted a better sighting so they crawled another hundred or so yards then Morgan had his confirmation, and at the same time he shook his head in exasperation because clearly, what the attackers had done after trying to catch Burt, and having the entire range crew come boiling back to help him, was duck down the slope on the east side where they would be out of sight, and ride southward.

Morgan said, "We better get Sut and Pete. Sure as I'm settin' here they're goin' down by the river." He did not have to add anything; the only reason their enemies would try to get ahead was because they knew Burt's crew would also go southward. The attackers would set up another ambush.

Burt went down the slope in disgust. He wanted to end this, get it over with. According to his lights those men should not have been able to trail them this far, nor as fast as they had. Like Morgan, and perhaps Pete and Sut as well, Burt wanted to force this running battle to a conclusion.

He saw Pete and Sut from above and made a night-bird call which they understood and called back, then he and Morg went on down, flopped back in the grass and explained what they had done and where they thought the attackers were.

Pete shook his head. "Damn it all, this could go on and on."

Burt disagreed. "Someone's got to ride back and fetch Morgan's horse." He looked directly at Pete. "I'll carry Morg double. The three of us'll go on down a ways and hunt up their ambush."

Pete was already arising to go after the horse when he said, "Burt, most folks who go lookin' for an ambush ride right into one."

Pete mounted his animal and turned it back up the canyon. The others watched him depart, then Morgan tugged up his trouser-leg to examine his knee. It was swollen and discoloured. He shoved the trouser-leg down and looked southward as far as he could see, which was not very far because of the uneven hillsides, then he stood up, ready to ride.

Burt and Morgan took the lead. They did not follow the trail out in the bottom of the canyon. Their enemies would have at least one spy up a sidehill somewhere waiting for that. They reined in as close to the east side as they could, and while they still were not adequately shielded from seeking eyes, at least until they got closer they would probably remain unseen.

Morg mumbled from behind Burt's saddle. "I never figured I'd see the day I wanted to see underbrush."

Burt did not answer. He was intently studying the easterly slope for a sign of someone watching from up there. But wherever the spy was, he would be hidden in tall grass, unless he stood up, and he'd be a fool to do that.

Burt knew every yard of the country they were passing over, which may have been an advantage but he did not feel that it was; not where visibility was unimpaired, providing moving objects were higher than a man's waist.

He thought as he rode along looking for the watcher. There were not many places men could establish an ambuscade, unless they abandoned their horses and got into position on foot. He thought about that, and regretted that he and Morgan had not crawled another mile or so over the top-out trail, because somewhere on ahead, perhaps on the east side of the rim, the attackers had had to tether their animals out of sight.

He pulled back to a halt studying the sidehill. Morgan leaned around Burt to also look up there. "You see him?" he asked.

Burt's answer was short. "No, but I got an idea. Their horses aren't on this side or we'd see them. They'll be down the far side."

Morgan pondered that until Sut came on up, right hand resting lightly on a gun stock as he too peered up the sidehill.

Burt said, "Sut and I'll climb up there, go over the top and find their horses. Morg, you stay down here and wait for Pete. You two fellers hide where you can, and wait."

Morgan scowled. "Wait for what?"

"Their horses to come back over the rim in a

rush. Afoot, we got 'em."

Sut wiped off sweat while considering the sidehill. It looked much steeper from down in the canyon than it actually was, but nevertheless, to a man who never climbed hills on foot, it remained formidable.

Sut looked around. "I like the other idea better; find their hidin' place and blow 'em out of it."

Burt's answer scotched Sut's argument. "And they'd duck back, get a-horseback again, and go farther along to set up another bushwhack. On foot, we can harry the bastards until they're ready to give up."

Burt swung to the ground and looked back. Sut dismounted, stiffly and reluctantly, pulled out his saddlegun and turned for another pained look up the tall-grass sidehill. "My maw used to say she didn't raise no idiots . . . I'd sure hate to have her see me right now."

As Burt started to turn Morgan leaned down and said, "You figure Pete and me should just set here?"

Burt looked up at the dusky face with its scrawny stubble and hard, obsidian eyes. Morgan was not going to just hide over here for an hour or two any more than he had obeyed Burt's injunction the night Burt had found the crawling horse thieves. He said, "Morg, they're waitin' and they're watching, and Pete's not able to be much help."

Then he turned, jerked his head at Sut and

they entered the buffalo-grass.

They did not have to crouch nor crawl up the hill, which was a blessing, but they had to halt often. Sut, like Pete, was built rock-like and strong, which was not the ideal structure for mountain-climbing. Also, he was not accustomed to doing something like this and ran out of wind easily.

The last time they halted, just under the top-out, and sank down to hide in the grass, Sut lifted his hat, swabbed off sweat, dropped the hat back down and looked irritably at the range-boss. "Burt," he solemnly said, "If cowboyin' is such a romantic occupation, how's it come there aren't more men in it? I'll tell you — there just plain aren't that many dumb damned fools." He craned around, eyed the rim, and sighed. "We better crawl from here."

They crawled, Burt's knees, already tender, felt every slight shift of land and almost every pebble. He came up over the rim like an Indian, inches up off his belly, head shoved out like the head of a turtle.

He saw the thin little trail on the far side but that was all he saw, so he turned southward, got back into the heavier trail along the rim and followed it until it veered eastward under the rim, then he dropped belly-down and lay a long while searching every yard of the darker area down the hill where that little turgid creek ran and where the underbrush and trees made shadows and protective barriers.

131

Sut lay beside him, face in the grass, sucking air and resting. Right at this moment Sut Sutherland did not give a copper-coloured damn if the horses were down there. He would not have roused up if Burt had leaned to tell him there was a solid gold rock down there as big as a cow.

It was a long wait, and when Burt eventually caught sight of something which held his interest, the movement came and went so briefly the rangeboss could only try and guess what had made it. But he had the locale in sight.

Sut roused himself to lie with his head propped upon one hand to also watch. The movement came again, briefly and unevenly. Sut raised up slightly, then said, "Horse shakin' his tail sure as I'm a foot high. Yonder in among those pines near that big bush below the cottonwood trees."

Burt knew the place because he had been watching it. Sut was probably correct about the source of that movement but Burt remained belly-down for a while longer, until he had seen the same movement two more times, then he began considering ways of getting down there unseen, in case the horses had someone among them with a carbine.

There was only one way to reach the far side of the slope and that was the same way he and Sut had got up from the opposite side. He looked around. "How are your knees?"

Sut answered promptly. "Sore."

"They wouldn't be if you hadn't been such an unregenerate sinner and had prayed more."

"What kind of a sinner?"

Burt turned back to measuring out the way they would have to crawl down there. "If someone's with those horses he's goin' to see us sure as hell." Burt turned that over in his mind then also said, "Shootin' up hill, a man can't ever be very accurate."

Sut's pained expression returned. "If you're so damned sure of that, you crawl ahead in the lead." He waited until Burt was gathering himself to start down through the tall grass then added another thought. "There sure was a hell of a lot no one told me about this ridin' job when I hired on, rangeboss."

Burt started over the top-out and down the far sidehill. He was hidden from anyone below, but he and Sut left a tell-tale trail behind where they pressed the grass flat. Sut looked back several times, noticed that, but did not worry as much about it as he worried about someone coming along the rim, seeing them down on all fours like a pair of cub bears, and shooting at them. They were very visible from back up along the top-out. He started to mention this to Burt, but the rangeboss changed course abruptly and Sut kept silent as he tried to guess why Burt had done that.

The reason was simple enough. The nearest underbrush which grew up the slope a hundred or so yards from the canyon's overgrown bottom, reached that high, and Burt wanted shelter even more than he wanted those drowsing, tethered horses.

Sut was dripping sweat by the time they got among the first bushes. It did not help, either, that they could now hear creek water trickling over stones.

But Burt turned southward, got up to his feet, ignoring the watercourse, and began sashaying back and forth through underbrush taller than he was, and Sut followed.

It was hot down in the overgrown canyon. Also, there were hundreds of gnats which seemed attracted to the pair of sweaty men. Sut muttered to himself as he stole along. Where they finally halted to listen, and heard horses stamping at flies or gnats not too far ahead. Sut leaned and said, "Don't stampede them all, or we're goin' to have to crawl back up and over that damned mountain."

Burt had the scent of sweaty horses long before he caught a glimpse of them standing in shadows perfectly camouflaged by speckled tree-shade and underbrush.

He went onward for another dozen or so yards then crept among a dense stand of thorny bushes, sank to one knee and by carefully parting the underbrush was able to see ahead.

The horses were dozing. They had been ridden hard, judging from their appearances, and were no doubt pleased to have this prolonged opportunity to rest. Flies were bothering them. They not only stamped but swung their tails and occasionally waggled their ears.

Burt looked for the man guarding them. Sut

got flat down to push his head out around the base of a big bush and seek the same man, but if he was up ahead, he was not in sight. Sut decided he might be down by the creek and pulled back to slip down and look. Burt did not move as his companion stealthily moved back, around, and stole away toward the sound of water. Burt thought the watcher might be up the sidehill, perhaps in the underbrush up there, but he could not find the man, and he could not even find a trail where a man had passed along to get up there.

Finally deciding the horse-guard might indeed be down by the creek where it would be cooler as well as shadier, Burt turned in that direction also.

He had little difficulty. Evidently there were a great variety of varmints who watered at that creek because there were innumerable little trails, along with some wider ones which had probably been made by deer or other large animals. He found a good, wide trail and went along it trying not to make a sound.

He did not see Sut and after passing mid-way along he could no longer see the tethered horses, although he could hear their occasional stamping sounds.

The gnats were thicker the closer he got to the water, perhaps because there was very little sunlight down there, because of the tall brush and trees. If there had been birds down here — and there most certainly had been — the arrival of the men with the horses had put them to flight. Burt did not hear a single bird as he finally came to the spongy ground, beyond which no underbrush grew, but which had pale, wet grass. Here, he saw the creek passing out of northward undergrowth, running past where he was standing, and going southward past brush and trees but about a hundred or so feet from either. He saw boot-tracks. They did not belong to Sut, they were the imprints of a taller man.

The tracks went southward as though the man who had made them wanted to go below the area where the horses had been watered. Burt shrugged about that. Most men seeking a drink of water went *above* where horses had drunk.

Then he saw Sut. Caught a glimpse of him upon the far side of the little creek where he whipped across a narrow clearing and got lost among the underbrush again. He was satisfied about one thing, the way Sut was moving, he was on a trail. Burt waited, then inched ahead to peer southward. He saw nothing down there, made a big bound, landed across the creek in more punky, grassy soil, and hastened up into the underbrush where he saw Sut's tracks, and turned to hasten after them.

13

A Struggle

Eagerness or carelessness caused Sut to make a mistake.

Burt was on his back-trail moving as swiftly as he dared, reasonably confident they had the advantage of surprise, when he heard an abrupt sound of metal clashing up ahead through the underbrush but on the creek-side. Then he heard a chain rattle briefly and a man's strangled gasp.

He pushed ahead, found Sut sitting on the ground, his carbine to one side leaning in a bush. Sut's face was taut with pain. Burt rushed up, saw the raccoon trap on Sut's ankle, and knelt to use both hands to spring it open so that Sut could withdraw his ankle. If Sut had not been wearing cowhide boots the jaws of the trap would have sunk deep through meat and muscle to the bone, as it was, with the trap removed, Sut rocked back and forth grinding his teeth in silent anguish.

Burt considered the trap. It had been pegged down as they usually were by a short length of chain, and it was rusty, so whoever had run a trapline down in here had not patrolled his layout in a long time, or perhaps, as often happened, the trapper had either overlooked this particular trap or had not been able to find it.

Burt pitched the thing aside and reached for Sut's leg. It was not broken at the ankle but that was not much consolation to Sutherland. He relaxed a little at a time, still with pain reflected in his face, and said, "Why didn't that son of a bitch down yonder step into it instead of me?"

Burt looked around. "Did you see him?"

"Yeah. In'ian. He was strollin' through the brush without any idea anyone was behind him. Tall redskin carryin' a carbine." Sut gestured. "Go after him. I'll be all right, but damn it I can't go with you."

Burt stood up gazing southward. Depending upon how far ahead the Indian was would determine whether or not he had heard the trap spring closed when Sut stepped into it.

Sut swore under his breath and gestured. "Hurry up. If we lose him. . . ."

Burt turned and started back through the underbrush. A fleeting thought occurred to him: Now, they would *have* to get hold of at least one horse because Sut would never be able to walk all the way back.

He did not see anyone but he found the fresh tracks of a man with large feet. It required a full fifteen minutes for him to locate the unsuspecting Indian. Fortunately the man had been so far

138

ahead of Sut he had not heard the trap spring closed.

When Burt finally saw him, the Indian had a saddlegun leaning against a scaly-barked pine tree and had a cigarette dangling from his lips as he stood with his head tilted watching a spiralling red-tailed hawk. The Indian had a sixgun and shellbelt around his middle. From the rear he looked like any other rangeman, and the way he was standing, slouched, bored acting, he clearly had no idea he was being stalked.

Burt had to restrain himself. There were a number of pines around this spot, which meant there was a lot of dead wood, brittle little rotting bits of pine-limb in the grass. He knew what would happen the moment he stepped on one of those things, and watched the ground even more closely as he skulked ahead than he watched the tall, lanky Indian.

He was discovered, but not because he snapped a twig, because the Indian flipped his smoke into the creek, picked up his carbine to cradle it in the bend of an arm, and started to turn. By that time Burt was close enough to club the man with his Winchester, and as the Indian came around Burt raised the gun with both hands and stopped moving so that when the Indian saw him, surprise would be complete.

It was. The Indian was a dark man, probably a full-blood. His black eyes had muddy whites and at one time he'd had smallpox; his face was scarred from it. When he met Burt's stare the Indian's nostrils flared. That was the only sign he offered that he had seen an enemy. He saw Burt one second, the very next second he hurled his carbine at Burt and leaned to go for his holstered Colt. Burt instinctively flinched aside, the flung saddlegun did not strike him but it ruined his aim even at that distance. But he fired. The reverberations were stifled as much by all the trees and underbrush as by the steep-standing canyon walls.

The Indian jumped, so Burt's bullet must have come close. He was frantically swinging his sixgun to bear when Burt did as the Indian had done. He flung the carbine, and he did not miss. But all the blow did was divert the tall Indian so that when his handgun went off Burt heard the big, clumsy slug go ripping through underbrush at least two yards to his left.

Burt sprang, struck the Indian's gunarm, hard, crossed over as the Indian staggered off-balance, and struck the Indian over the heart with all his force. The Indian sagged, his mouth dropped open, but he did not go down so Burt brought up a knee. The Indian had enough sense to twist. Burt's knee struck the man's hip. He saw the gunarm rising again and aimed a vicious kick. He missed the wrist, kicked the gun completely out of the tall Indian's grip, and whirled to finish off his adversary, but the redskin was tougher than Burt thought, he turned to absorb blows along his left side, then turned back with a looping big overhand hay-maker of a blow, grazed Burt's shoulder and stopped the range-boss's forward momentum.

For a pair of seconds they stood sucking air and staring at one another, then the Indian snarled and lunged, caught cloth and struggled to get both long, sinewy arms around the rangeboss in back. He did not pin both Burt's arms to his side, which was a mistake because Burt got the cup of one hand under the Indian's jaw and as the squeezing arms tightened like steel to force out Burt's wind, the Indian's head was being steadily forced back. Finally, with the Indian unwilling to release his grip even though his head was back as far as it could go, Burt swiftly released his cupped hold and smashed the fist across the redskin's gullet. It was not a powerful blow; Burt could not step back to get the range and momentum for that, but across a man's unprotected throat it was adequate. The Indian's locked fists turned loose, his arms dropped and he made gagging sounds as he stepped back.

He was bringing a hand up to his throat when Burt fired a poised right hand. It caught the Indian squarely upon the slant of the jaw. The Indian fell like a log.

Burt eyed his fallen adversary for a moment, then turned toward the creek to drink and sluice water over his head. It ran down both front and back of his shirt; the process of evaporation would help cool him off.

He went back, unloaded the unconscious

man's two guns, briefly frisked him for hide-out weapons, then left him to hasten across the creek where the horses were standing, lead three of them back across, and left one by the unconscious man while he rode one and led the last one back to Sut.

When he got there Sut was standing upright with the aid of a crooked deadfall little pine limb, his expression showing anxiety. "What happened?" he asked, and Burt gestured toward the led-horse. "Get astride. We got a cold-cocked redskin down yonder. I want to get him gagged and tied before we head out of here."

Sut rode back but had to sit his saddle and watch Burt do all the work, and that lanky Indian was a lot of solid dead weight to hoist up off the ground and atop a horse. He was beginning to regain consciousness, too, but as Sut balanced him in the saddle Burt tied the man's arms behind his back, tied his two empty weapons to the saddle, then, with the venomous black eyes upon him, he used the Indian's neckerchief to gag the prisoner with. He had no intention of riding out of there, in the direction of the Indian's friends, and have the captive cry out a warning.

By the time they were ready to start picking their way down the canyon Burt was sweating again.

There was one horse left, and while it had been Burt's intention to stampede the horses, now that they were riding three of them there was no point in spooking the fourth animal. He trailed along behind Sut, perfectly content to be a follower.

Burt led the way, the captive was behind him, and Sut was behind the captive. Finding a place to break out of the canyon required time. In fact before Burt found a way out, short of riding straight up, across the top-out and down the far side — where they would be in plain sight of Morgan and Pete as well as of the other men hiding down there somewhere — the sun was beginning to slant away, Sut was both impatient and in pain, and the sidehill did not really begin to slant southward until the trees and under-brush gave way to grass. Then, Burt found a number of game trails.

They made a roundabout ride across the fat haunch of hillside, halted where Burt wanted to scout ahead on foot, and did not resume their way until he returned, nodded to Sut and without a word swung up and struck out again.

The Indian watched the country, but most of his concentration was upon the back of the man who had beaten him senseless. Sweat ran down his face, he could not push it off, and he was probably thirsty as well because both Sut and Burt were before they started around the south slope, Burt well ahead and riding alertly. Somewhere ahead, were the ambushers. Burt had no idea where they could be and he could not afford to make a mistake.

Very distantly he heard cattle lowing, not very

many and only occasionally, so neither he nor Sut paid much attention. Otherwise, that slanting sun was still well above the westerly rims, over across the canyon, which meant there would be excellent visibility for a while yet, and that in turn meant that three mounted men riding through tall grass would be discernible the moment they completed rounding the sloping hillside.

Burt halted, took his reins back to Sut, ignored the Indian and started ahead on foot again, but this time in order to be less of a target, he moved swiftly, in spurts, and ran crouched over.

Thirst was more of a torment than an actual discomfort. For a while he was able to forget it entirely when he finally had the canyon trail in sight, dropped down to inch forward through the grass and study the empty land ahead. There was a wide, long curve, which limited Burt's view, but even so if there had been trouble up around the bend he would have picked up the sound of it, and he heard nothing.

He crept ahead again, travelling around the sidehill until he was progressing northward, on up the canyon to get beyond the obstructing bulge of mountainside.

A very large, fat greeny snake, hiding from the heat, suddenly glided directly across in front of the crawling rangeboss and Burt's hair rose up, but the snake did not even look around in his haste. Burt used the next moment to shake off sweat and peer around for the snake's mate; a prevalent belief in range country was that snakes, particularly rattlers, travelled in pairs.

But there was no second reptile and Burt eased ahead, carefully for a dozen or so yards, and then with less caution and more curiosity.

Finally, where he could see northward up the canyon, and off to his right up the grassed-over slope, he detected a narrow fresh trail. Men, he told himself, had made that trail, probably by crawling one behind the other. He traced its length to a particularly flourishing stand of tall, very dark green grass, surmised there might be a seepage-spring up there, and also guessed that was where the ambushers would be, since the trail went directly to that dark green place and did not appear to go any farther.

He sat back to ponder. If those bushwhackers were still over there, then they had the patience of saints because by Burt's guess he and Sut had been gone about two hours. If they had got tired of waiting and had gone up the canyon north-ward, Morgan and Pete would have seen them, most likely, and there should have been gunfire.

The alternative to speculating about all this was to crawl over closer to that dark green site. He started ahead. Far back, it would be up to Sut to watch their captive and stay out of sight. Burt had all the confidence in the world in Sutherland, even with a hurting and swollen an-kle.

He got to the green area, inched along on all fours like a stalking wolf, parted thick grass to peer ahead, went still closer repeating this until he could see where men had crushed down the grass, but now there were no men there.

He covered the last twenty feet, emerged into the place where the ambushers had waited, and would have gone across to the far side in search of another fresh trail, when a gunshot suddenly sounded, its ricochetting echoes bouncing back and forth across the canyon.

He waited for more shooting but there was none so he started ahead again, had covered another half-dozen yards and stopped stone-still when gunfire suddenly blasted the stillness, this time the deeper, more cannon-like thunder of sixguns intermingling with flatter, more waspish sound of carbines.

He guessed that either the ambushers had found Pete and Morgan, or had been found by Pete and Morgan, but in either case his range-riders were out gunned so he got up into a crouch and ran toward the sounds of gunfire.

He saw three terrified horses fighting their hobbles, and up closer to the slope in the grass he saw puffs of gunsmoke where two hidden men were firing up the sidehill. Up there, it was impossible to guess how many men were firing back from the same poor cover, but he guessed it was either three or four men.

He dropped down, waited for a fresh puff of smoke, then levered up and fired three time as fast as he could, one bullet to the centre beneath that powder smoke, one to the left of it and one